NO BADGE REQUIRED
A JAKE MORGAN THRILLER

W.L. RIPLEY

WOLFPACK
PUBLISHING
— EST 2013 —

Published in the United States by Wolfpack Publishing, Las Vegas

Wolfpack Publishing
5130 S. Fort Apache Road, 215-380
Las Vegas, NV 89148

wolfpackpublishing.com

Paperback ISBN: 978-1-63977-009-0
eBook ISBN: 978-1-63977-008-3

NO BADGE REQUIRED

ACKNOWLEDGEMENTS

Thanks to my brother Lt. James Ripley (Missouri State Highway Patrol) for his input regarding crime scene forensic procedures and jurisdictional matters.

Life is a long preparation for something that never happens.

W.B. Yeats

CHAPTER 1

Texas Ranger Lieutenant Jake Morgan almost didn't see the guy in time because he was thinking about her again.

Jake had staked out the loading dock for three days, squinting through the heat shimmers rising from the endless plain, thinking West Texas is the fucking moon. There had been trucks docking and leaving this isolated location with truck plates from places as far away as Illinois and several from Mexico. It was a cartel operation from the looks of it, and though Jake wanted to bust up the operation he was more intent on finding the cartel soldier who killed Umberto Segundo, a Texas Ranger with three children and a good friend to Jake.

Texas promoted and transferred Missouri born Jake to Company E from Company B. He had liked Company B which was Dallas and things to do. A raise came with the promotion, but he wondered where they thought he could spend the extra bucks in a place normal humanity had abandoned? He hesitated to take the promotion as his heart was back in Missouri with a young lady who opened up parts of him he thought didn't exist or at least had gone dormant.

He sat in a dry arroyo with the desert wind swirling and throwing caliche dust into his face and all he could think of was a young woman with a great sense of humor back in his hometown and how they had been apart too long.

Her name was Harper Bannister. She was not returning his calls and that was on his mind. His promise to Harper was a return within the month which was four months ago, but all that was before the cartel shot and crippled his friend, Texas Ranger, Umberto Segundo. Segundo had a wife and three kids and Jake was determined to take down the operation that had cost his friend the use of his legs.

Since transferring to Troop E, Jake had 27 cold case files on his desk, worked nine homicides, three Ranger officer involved shootings all justified, twelve child kidnappings and the murder of an ICE agent. He had been working wall-to-wall and traveling extensively and his social life was non-existent. Every time he thought about getting in touch with Harper it seemed he would be called away by one of these things, and now he was in charge of this team working to turn off the flow of cocaine of a Mexican cartel and take down Segundo's shooter.

These things were on his mind and king-hell lucky when he heard the scratch of Velcro when the man pulled his weapon, and even luckier when the handgun caught on the man's shirt.

Jake rolled and cleared his service weapon, a SIG Sauer .357, as the Mexican fumbled with his over-large six shooter. Jake leveled the SIG, shouted, "Texas Ranger," and then heard the report of the big revolver. A round kicked up dirt by Jake's hip as he double tapped the SIG striking the man in the chest and right nipple.

That's when the second round from another source sawed off a palm of the Comanche Prickly Pear Jake had been using to obscure his observation point.

The second shooter fired too quickly and sprayed another round before Jake shot him in the throat. The man tripped and slid heavily into the arroyo, rolled down the bank, choking and gagging, spraying blood onto the hard Texas clay.

Jake was amped with adrenaline and his heart was talking to him, but he got things under control and checked the vitals of both men. They were both DRT.

That done, he became aware of the burning in his hip and reached down and felt the wetness of blood.

Jake called in and within an hour he heard the sound of trucks firing up as he raised to peer over the edge of the bank and saw two Safety Department units pluming dust, and in the distance heard the sound of chopper blades before he sighted the Airbus AS350 helicopter with the 'TEXAS DPS' logo under the belly of the chopper.

Two men died at Jake's hand and not even the first this month.

Well, hell. His captain wasn't going to like any of this, but the second man, the one Jake shot in the throat, turned out to be the guy who shot Segundo in the back.

***

Jake was right, his captain didn't like it.

"I'm getting heat from Austin," said his captain. "And shit rolls downhill so now you're going to get some. Morgan, if you're not beating some guy senseless, you're shooting them. Your reputation, while your drinking buddies may find it entertaining, is not well thought of by people who fund our little organization, and I realize you wanted to square things for Umberto." The captain paused to take a breath and then said. "Do you know what they call you, and don't give me your bored look! I know you don't care, but they're calling you John Wesley Morgan. You get that?"

What was Jake supposed to say to that?

Jake said, "I was returning fire. Captain, forensics dug a .45-70 shell from the bank and also the 9mm round that nicked me." Could you believe it, thought Jake, who carries a .45-70 Colt sidearm these days? The Cartel thugs are getting colorful and nostalgic. And the hip wound kept him awake at night as he didn't like the painkillers nor the Ambien the doctors prescribed, and refused to take. "I tried to cuff them while they were shooting at me, but they weren't having it."

"Don't be flippant, Morgan. I've been in Public Safety for 25 years and never pulled my weapon."

"So, you've never been in that situation, right?" Wondering now how his captain had any experience that allowed him to criticize.

The captain made a face, placed both hands on the edge of the desk and pushed his chair back. "Both men were Hispanic. How do you think that looks?"

"I'll make sure to shoot two Caucasians next, try to even things up." The men were working for a Mexican Cartel, what country did the captain think they were from? Getting harder to deal with the daily horrors Jake was seeing in Southwest Texas let alone being harangued for defending himself. "Maybe have me work white collar crime, more white guys."

Captain didn't think that was funny. What could you do? Never mind that Ranger Umberto Segundo was Hispanic himself.

"Ranger policy calls for an administrative leave of absence, so take your vacation and get the hell out of my office. I'll call you when I'm over being pissed off at you. Besides, you need to let that wound heal. You're a fine Ranger and you have important work to do here but when you get back, we're going to discuss the situation going forward and some adjustments in your law enforcement style."

But Jake knew as soon as he left the captain's office he was never coming back. He was done with West Texas and shadowy border outlaws with automatic weapons and Wild West revolvers who had no compunction about using them.

They could just kill each other without him.

CHAPTER 2

Wednesday morning, two weeks after his return to Missouri, Jake Morgan, now Paradise County Investigator Morgan, got a call on a body reported by a farmer. She was nobody and that's how they had treated her, dumping her lifeless body in a dirt road ditch south of the city of Paradise off route 7. Dispatch said the med techs were on route.

He was back home again, what he called home anyway, in Paradise, Missouri, where Jake had played high school sports, gaining some recognition as a high school quarterback and a two guard on a basketball team that won 25 games and won the district tournament his senior year.

Paradise was once a two-route Norman Rockwell town with second-generation oak trees now swallowed up by progress and bypassed by an interstate highway and divided into two distinct demographics – the long-established generation of Paradise citizens and the bedroom community. Standing firmly astride both entities was the Nouveau Riche entrepreneurs and land-grabbers who had moved in and taken over when Vernon Mitchell died and his holdings seized save for those which his son, Alex, managed to preserve.

Jake arrived at the homicide site and parked his vehicle, a Ford Explorer badged with the emblem of the Paradise County Sheriff, far back from the crime scene to avoid contamination of tire tracks. The sun worked its magic, warming him as he walked, an ironically beautiful day which contrasted with the darkness of the morning's task.

Already on-site was the County Medical Examiner, Dr. Ezekial Montooth, a guy Jake had played basketball with in high school, a good friend from the old days, and Sheriff's Deputy Gretchen Bailey. They were standing far back from the body like Jake had instructed.

"I took a few pictures on my cell," Bailey said, when Jake arrived. She wore the county uniform and a baseball cap, a ponytail hanging behind the cap. Bailey was good help and of all the deputies, Jake trusted her the most. There were other deputies who were tougher and better shots, but Bailey was smart, meticulous and got things done due to her C.J. training at Central Missouri University.

"I'll need some from all four angles, also any tire tracks including those from your vehicles. I would like some professional photos, also. Did you call Wiley?" Wiley was the photographer the county used.

"He's on the way," Bailey said.

Jake nodded at her and said, "Nobody touched anything, right?"

"No."

Jake looked at Dr. Ezekial Montooth and raised an eyebrow.

"I didn't touch anything, Morgan," said the M.E. "So, how about it with the stink eye."

"Zeke the Shiek," Jake said, brightly. "Good to see you, buddy."

Dr. Zeke was a tall, angular man, with longish wavy hair, a weather-worn St. Louis Cardinals hat sideways on his head, and wearing faded olive-colored scrubs. He had a half-smoked cigarette hanging from the corner of his mouth.

"When you care enough to send the very best, I'm your man." Zeke fished another cigarette from a pack of Marlboros.

"When are you going to quit smoking?" Jake said.

"When you do."

"I quit two days ago and all this time I thought you

were a better quitter than I am."

Zeke tossed a pebble at Jake. "And so it starts. Can we do some work?"

Jake took a sip of the convenience store coffee that tasted like it was brewed for King Tut.

"I've got some crime scene tape in my unit," Bailey said.

"Mark it off large," Jake said. "Bigger than you might think would be big enough; we can always make it smaller. After that, call in and get help out here. I want to know if anyone in the area heard or saw anything. It's pretty remote but you never know."

"What do you think?" Jake asked Dr. Zeke.

Zeke leaned in and said, "Hard to tell until I get her on the table. How long before I can move her?"

Jake gently rolled the body to look underneath. "Wiley, get some photos, please? All angles and different distances; close-up, moderate about 10 feet and long distance. Get the tire tracks and any footprints. You can blow these up as needed, right? Zeke here will want some for his bedroom wall."

"Lame," Dr. Zeke said.

Photographer Wiley arrived and took photos from four angles and three distances – distant, moderate and close-up. That done, Jake approached the body slowly, careful of his footsteps, and examined the ground for anything unusual to the scene. Jake produced some plastic baggies and began bagging some things he found on the ground. Finally, Jake and Zeke moved to the body and gave it a closer look. The medical unit arrived, and Jake had them stand down.

"Zeke, do you know how cops and doctors are alike?" Jake said, kneeling to take a look at the ground around the body.

Zeke made a face and shook his head. "No."

"They both want to be policemen when they grow up."

"Gee," Zeke said, as he and Jake slowly inched closer to the body. "I forgot how fucking hilarious you think you are."

"Easy to forget when I'm not around to help you out."

Wiley chuckled and began snapping photos.

Jake saying to Zeke now, "She's dressed expensively, but not rich herself. They left the rings on, the diamonds are real, and so robbery wasn't the motive. She's been taken care of by someone, a sugar daddy, but he stopped. The killer may even be the person gave her the jewelry."

"How do you know that?"

"As I said, the rings are real, the clothes are expensive, but the colors are starting to fade and there's some fraying at the hemline. She's had an expensive hair treatment, looks like subtle highlights, but the roots are growing out."

"You're a regular Sherlock Holmes," Zeke said.

When Deputy Bailey finished marking the crime scene off, Jake said to her, "You any good with artwork?"

"I'm not too bad."

"Get a pad and sketch the scene; include measurements if you could. I have a tape measure in my car. On your sketch, leave Doc here out of it, we don't want to scare anybody."

"I feel a smart remark coming on," Zeke said.

"It'll have to come from Bailey," Jake said, smiling. "Long as I've known you, I haven't heard much in the way of smart."

"It's just a wonderful event to have you back, Jake," Dr. Zeke said.

"Good to see you, too, Zeke."

Two more deputies arrived, and Jake put them to work canvassing the homes nearby to see if anyone heard or saw anything. "Just ask what they remember about the time frame, did they hear dogs bark, car engines start up, did they remember waking up and looking at the clock for no apparent reason. How long have they lived there, have they ever had any issues with neighbors or know of any? Those kinds of things. Document names and get phone numbers."

After Jake was satisfied with the photos and bagged cigarette butts, candy wrappers, and a beer can, which may or may not have been there for days, Jake pulled on a pair of latex gloves and picked through her purse and found lip gloss, no cash, and a cocktail napkin that read 'Paradise Country Club'. "No I.D., but we can fingerprint her. Somebody will need to contact the family."

"I can do that," Bailey said.

"Thanks, Bailey. Also, as delicately as possible, try to ascertain where they were overnight."

Bailey nodded.

Zeke rolled the woman's head for a better look and said, "I think I know this girl; Cynthia Cross is her name. She has signs of hyperthermia, and bit through her tongue suggesting seizure or part of the trauma inflicted." Dr. Zeke rolled latex gloves from his hands and gave Jake an appraising look. "You've seen this kind of thing before, haven't you?"

"Yeah."

"That's what I heard. You were a Texas Ranger and now you're with us?"

"Doesn't add up, does it?"

"Well, glad you're back, but it's a weird career move. I'm a doctor and see a lot of death but not like this. Doesn't get easier, you know, seeing this."

"You're right about that."

"Some livor mortis on her backside," Zeke said. "She has been rolled over."

Jake kneeled beside the body, his elbows on his knees. "The killer didn't want to see her face," Jake said, without emotion. He reached down and gently pressed on the purplish discoloration on the woman's back and the area turned pale but discolored when he released. "He knew her. Roll her over and let's see the other side."

The two men gently rolled the body, careful not to disturb anything under the body that could become evidence.

"See the red dots in her eyes?" Zeke said.

Jake nodded. "He strangled her." Jake looked closer and noticed the raw red worm that had cut into the skin of her throat. Jake pointed at the abrasion and said, "Looks like the killer started to strangle her with something like a necklace but it broke." Looking around now to see if he could find whatever made the marks, or some fragment.

When he didn't find anything, Jake decided that the killer had taken the necklace with him for some reason.

Zeke dusted his pants with gloved hands and then said, "The blood has not fully congealed and there was livor mortis on the back. Dead less than eight hours, maybe less than four."

"She's attractive. The killer was careful with her face, she was turned over but there's no scrapes on her face. He held her face in hand when he turned her. She only has one earring."

"Yeah."

"Where's the other one? And the necklace that made those marks. Maybe he kept souvenirs."

"What kind of person does that?"

"Murderers, rapists and serial killers." Jake stood and looked down at the corpse and said, "Also, love starved M.E.s."

Dr. Zeke showed Jake a middle finger.

Jake smiled and said, "This is some sad shit. I better get over to the Country Club and see what I can stir up there."

"I don't envy you going out there, they are not going to like being associated with..." Zeke nodded at the body, "With this. Even if they're not involved, they'll want it quiet. There are some powerful people out there and you're not a favorite."

Jake shrugged. "Goes with the job and piss on them if they can't take a joke."

Zeke nodded. "Yeah, good luck, buddy."

"Thanks for getting here quickly, Zeke."

"You need anything else from me, Jake?" Bailey asked.

Jake nodded at the deceased and said, "Find out where she lives and seal it off. We'll need to go through that stuff."

CHAPTER 3

Harper Bannister checked her cell phone; the electronic print said, 'Jake Morgan', wh sich was the third in the last two days. She had gotten similar calls when she was in Colorado and while she was tempted to answer or call back, very tempted in fact, the fact Jake had disappeared for three months without a word and she was not ready to relent prevented her. Harper was not a vindictive person but when Jake returned to Texas, she was told he needed to get his stuff ready to move and give the Texas Department of Safety his notice of resignation.

And now days dissolved into months, and at first, she tried to understand he was busy, but four months was hard to take. She knew he was back in town working for Sheriff Buddy Johnson now, but Harper had already moved on, at least in her head, if not in her heart.

Harper had made the biggest mistake of her life, marrying Tommy Mitchell, and was going to be careful this time. She had married Tommy because he seemed exciting and perhaps a small rebellion against her father, Police Chief Cal Bannister, but soon after she became Mrs. Tommy Mitchell, the glow wore off and she found herself mired in a relationship with a controlling man who drank too much and strayed often. Once was too often.

Like her father, Jake was a law enforcement officer, and there were other resemblances – Both had a way of turning off all outside distractions when in pursuit of their profession, including the distractions posed by a teenaged girl and in Jake's case, a fully-realized woman in her early twenties.

She loved Jake and maybe she always had since the days as a prepubescent girl in tennis shoes who had a little girl crush on a brooding high school athlete who, to Harper, was a cross between James Dean and Brad Pitt. Jake wasn't what you would call shiver-handsome, and definitely not in Brad Pitt's range, but he had charisma and a fierce individuality that she could *feel* as if an invisible shield that both drew her to him and kept him distant from people, that is, everyone except Buddy Johnson and her high school teacher, Leo Lyons, who was Jake's other best friend.

This time, Mr. Jake Morgan would have to come after her, really come after her, and he wasn't going to get any breaks. He needed to prove his commitment.

She had a date that evening and needed to get ready. She was not excited at the prospect of a night out, even though the guy was wealthy and took her to these great places. But she didn't want fancy dinners and exotic vacations; she wanted...well, there it was.

Out loud, she said, "Damn you, Jake Morgan, for making me care."

***

It was four PM when Jake arrived at the Paradise Country Club, built by new money and protected by generations of Paradise Gentry, which included an Arnold Palmer lay-out for the golf course and two swimming pools. The clubhouse was hushed with expensive carpeting, festooned with Callaway drivers and TaylorMade irons and a large club lounge boasting signed golf prints of Rory McIlroy and Tommy Fleetwood. Every year the course hosted a Pro Seniors Golf tournament which had attracted names like Vijay Singh and John Daly. Jake had played the course on occasion though the green fees were pricey. Jake had a club membership he'd won on a golfing bet with a man who was subsequently murdered by his daughter-in-law.

Paradise County and its eponymously named county seat, fronted by the landmark WW2 statue, was defined by its past and its present, the town square still a main focus though storefronts were moving to the highway as a lot of money had been shoveled into Paradise County in recent years. The KC Star called Paradise, also the name of the county, the "biggest little town" in the Midwest. Paradise had grown from a sleepy two route town, when Jake was the quarterback for the high school team, to a thriving county seat that tripled in size and money while Jake was away in Texas. It was now two different demographic groups – the small-town people who had lived and died in Paradise and the Nouveau Riche who ran things. Jake returned home to find the place far different than he remembered. Like John Lennon said, "some things change forever, not for better".

Yet, the vibrations and ambiance of his halcyon days lingered in Jake's head like a fine cabernet.

Jake was met at the parking lot of the Country Club by his best friend, Sheriff Buddy Johnson, which didn't surprise him.

"Go slow in there, Jake," Buddy said.

"I can hardly wait to get in there and start shaking things up, you know, busting the fat-cat elitist swine." He smiled at Buddy. "How many of those guys you think voted for you?" said Jake looking up at Buddy, a large man who had kept many defenders off Jake back in their high school days at Paradise High School.

"More than you think," Buddy said. "I ran unopposed but now that you're on the team there will be regret voting for a black man who would hire an asshole for an investigator. And it wouldn't kill you to wear the badge occasionally."

"It pokes holes in my shirt."

"It's a clip-on."

"I forgot."

"It's a good thing I like you, because you're a lot of

trouble."

"I'm a troublemaker?"

Buddy snorted. "It's funny you think you're not."

The first person Jake wanted to interview was the bartender, Lanny 'The Lemon' Wannamaker, while Buddy talked to the club program director to get a list of who had been on hand for the party and possible contact numbers.

Jake found Lanny cleaning up the bar area. First thing he said was, "We're closed."

"Now you're open," Jake said. "You ever use lemon juice to bring out the blond, or just use the bottle stuff?"

"What do you want, Morgan?"

"You serving last night?" Jake said.

"Is this an official visit? I don't see a badge."

"I got one, but I only take it out for important people, and you don't qualify. What's your answer?"

"Yeah, I was here, what's this about?"

"I'll need a list of folks in attendance last night."

"Are you going to tell me what's going on?"

"You gonna get me a list or what?"

"You got a warrant?"

"I can get one but that'll just annoy me, and I'll have to drag you to town and make you wait until I get around to you." He stared deadpan at the bartender for several moments. "And sometimes I get really busy."

Wannamaker's mouth worked and he rubbed a bar towel between his hands. "Take it easy, Jake, damn, you're a rude person. I thought you were living in Texas."

"Now I'm here. How many people last night?"

"I didn't count 'em."

"Guess."

"I don't know, twenty or so."

"Was this a group or just the regular crowd?"

Lanny picked up a glass and began to rub it with a bar towel. "Just some people."

Jake was quiet again, waited.

"Okay," Lanny said, who stopped rubbing on the bar, "it was a group of people come in here once a month, sometimes more, the kind of people who can get me fired, dammit."

"See, was that so hard? I want your cash register tickets from last night, you know, the one's that lists who used a card."

"These guys put it on their club tab and pay with their monthly dues. They tip in cash."

"Still want it and a list of club members with recent bar tabs. Also, I want to see your security camera videos from last night."

"Well..."

"I can get a court order if you need one."

"That's not it," Wannamaker said. "They were turned off."

"Why did you turn them off, Lanny?"

"I didn't and I don't know who did. When I came in this morning, I went to check them, and the camera was turned off."

"Do you have a time when they went off?"

"Yeah, 7:07 last night."

Jake cocked his head a half-inch before saying, "I'm trying to imagine why anyone would happen to turn off the security cameras on this particular night. Was there a stripper hired to entertain?"

"That's against club rules."

"There you go, answering questions I didn't ask, which always makes me wonder if people are hiding something when they do that. You wouldn't be hiding something, would you, Lanny? Come on, was there a stripper here last night?"

"Am I under suspicion for something?"

"Not yet but avoid answering again or tell me about the club rules and I'll see what I can do to help you focus. Let's see here," Jake opened a small notepad and pretended to read from it. "What do you know, you're on probation, right?"

"Fuck, Jake," Wannamaker said, lifting a hand in supplication and looking around for help in the room. "You're so hostile. Why come at me with that?"

Jake crossed his arms and stared impassively at the

bartender. Waited again.

Wannamaker began rocking back-and-forth, deciding. Finally, he said, "Man, give me a break, I was told to keep that shit quiet. I could lose my job."

"That'd be a shame. Probably take them the better part of an hour to find a replacement. How much they give you?"

"A grand."

Jake whistled. "That's a lot," Jake said. Funny they paid a bartender that much for one night, Jake thinking they wanted his silence, but entertaining the boys with a naked dancer might be a reason. "Sounds like they wanted something in return besides building martinis. So, you did your part and didn't tell the club boss but the stripper's dead."

"Cynthia's dead? Shit." Wannamaker put a hand to his forehead.

"So, you did know she was here, even knew her name."

"I don't know nothing about any violence, man, I'm a peace-lover, I hate violence, you know. She was here and she was fine when I left."

"'When you left'? Why does the bartender leave before the party's over?"

"They told me they'd take care of it, and I could go home."

"Wow, you're a trusting guy, but a G-note buys a lot, I guess." He winked at Lanny. "Always wanted to say G-note. Get out a pen and something to write on and give me all the names you can think of were here last night and that's everybody. You do know how to spell, right?"

"How about it with the insults?"

"Part of my routine and I'm not charging you for the daytime show. Write it down, including the time you left and if you can remember when anyone else left. Who locked up?"

"You know him, was your old buddy, Jimmy Davenport."

CHAPTER 4

Jimmy Davenport was a high school teammate, like Dr. Zeke, and almost a friend back in high school, which was ten years ago now, but they fell out when Jake beat him out for a spot on the basketball team and a girl came between them, Rhonda Fuller, a cheerleader, who had a crush on Jake and Jimmy married her. Why is it always about a woman?

Davenport inherited his father's real estate holdings and turned them into a Holiday Inn out on the interstate, two convenience stores, a restaurant, and developed an upscale housing development. Davenport was smart and had done all right for himself, but Jake knew him well and realized nothing would ever be enough for Jimmy.

Jake again tried to call Harper but either she was out of cell tower range, or she didn't want to talk to him. Out of tower range was what he told himself so he wouldn't have to face the reality that it was the latter and that she was blowing him off. Women, huh? But she had a reason, he understood that, but it didn't make him feel better.

He called Davenport and asked if he could come by his office, and Jimmy offered to meet him for lunch at his new restaurant. "You'll like it, Jake, it's going to be a money maker."

Davenport's restaurant, The Homestead, was a cut above the usual fare in small communities and while a notch below elegant, it was warm, clean, and well-appointed. Jimmy greeted him with a firm handshake that lasted too long, flashed big teeth and favored Jake with a used car salesman smile.

"Jake Morgan, so very good to see you, old sport."

Jake nodded and said, "Jimmy."

"I married Rhonda," Jimmy said, the first thing out of his mouth when they were seated.

"Yeah, I heard."

"Man, I hate it we got crossways on that."

"Yesterday's news, Jimmy, I'm happy for you."

"Well, she divorced me."

"Sorry to hear that."

Jimmy unbuttoned his navy blazer and put an arm across the back of the booth, relaxed and folksy. "It's okay, I found someone new. Order the Manhattan to start off, best in the area, they use those custom ice shapes. On me."

"I'm on the clock, but thanks."

Jimmy ordered a dirty martini, Jake wondering why not the Manhattan, but it was like Jimmy to not take his own advice.

"When did you get back in town? I heard you were some kind of Texas Ranger or something."

"Was, made some changes, been back a couple weeks. I'm working for Buddy Johnson and Cal Bannister."

"The sheriff and the chief of police? Both?"

"It's a deal they worked out."

The color drained from Jimmy's face. "You're not dressed like a cop. Where's your badge?"

Jake stifled the impulse to haul out a cliché about not needing 'no stinkin' badge'. Jake shrugged instead. "Part of the deal is I don't have to wear a uniform, or a hat." Davenport looked at him and as a way of further explanation, Jake added, "I'm not really an accessories guy."

Davenport reached up and touched his nose. "Is this an official visit?"

"Doesn't have to be. Look, Jimmy, I need your help on something, there was a party of some kind at the country club and..."

"The girl, right?" Shaking his head now. "Knew they shouldn't have brought the stripper in. Look, it was just a...you know, a stag party; people and guys got a little drunk. So, maybe they broke a few club rules and maybe a couple county regs about, you know, nudity, but we didn't hurt anybody."

"Did you know her?"

"I may have seen her, you know, around."

"So, you did see her 'around' at the club, but you don't know her, right?"

Davenport shrugged. "Yeah."

"Do you think I'm here to enforce morality laws?"

Davenport knit his brow and said, "Why are you here?"

"She's dead and maybe gang raped," Jake said, hitting Jimmy with it straight on, looking for a reaction, a gambler's tell but got nothing. Jimmy was one of those guys who put you at ease, was a good salesman, but there was always something about him that made Jake hesitant to believe everything Jimmy said. "You know anything about that?"

"Hang on, Jake." He lifted a hand, palm out at Jake, to stop him. His face had colored. "I don't know anything about...that. Gang bang, wow. Look, I left early and I...I knew they were bringing one in, a stripper I mean and... damn, that's a lot, nobody there had anything to do with anything like that. There were some great people there."

"The kind of great people that bring in a stripper?" Jake said, deadpan, watching Jimmy's eyes. "Real pillars of the community?"

"Actually, they are."

"So, tell me how they came to be there hours before a young woman ends up dead and tossed in a ditch. Jimmy, you're dissembling, and I don't understand that if nothing is wrong. You want to back up a bit and try to get on an honest level with an old friend."

"You're not acting like an old friend, you're acting like –."

"Like a homicide investigator? You said you locked the place up."

"What? No...well, yeah, I went home and then had to come back to lock up because I promised I'd do that. But I did leave earlier like I said."

"What time did you leave the first time?"

Jake watched Jimmy cut his eyes to the left before he said, "I'm thinking it was about, I don't know, around eleven."

"When did you go back?"

"Two maybe or around then." Not sure of it or was he not sure he wanted to give an exact time.

"Anybody still there when you arrived?"

"Just the clean-up guy?"

"Why didn't he lock up?"

"Fuck, I don't know, I promised I'd see it got locked up, so I did. He's not that trustworthy so I sent him home."

"So, you hire a janitor who isn't trustworthy? Were you afraid the guy would steal the booze or some other reason? Who are some of these 'great people', you know, the pillars?"

Davenport blew air between his lips. "Aw, c'mon, Morgan." Now he was 'Morgan'. "You're scratching at something that's not going anywhere and is just going to create shit storm for us both, and, well, that's your job I guess and you're too smart for that right? But this...this is a terrible thing and it'll just blow up. The people I'm talking about are...well, like I said, really outstanding citizens."

"Name some of them."

"Well, I didn't know all of them."

Watching Davenport's eyes now Jake decided Davenport did know them, Jake was sure of it. Was he afraid or was he complicit?

"Keep being evasive, Davenport, that doesn't set off my spider sense or anything." If Jake was 'Morgan' then Jimmy was now 'Davenport'. Jake reached into his shirt pocket and produced the folded paper where Lanny Wannamaker had written some names. Jake unfolded it and said, "Names are right here. I see a judge, a Medfield big shot, a senator, a doctor, couple others and well, what do you know, here's your name. Who are these people, Davenport?"

"You seem to know everything which tells me you already have the answers and now you're pushing."

"It's no fun to ask questions when you don't have the answers, that way I know who to trust and who'll lie to me. You wouldn't lie to me, would you? Was this a group or a service club party?"

"Well, yeah, it was a bunch of guys who meet Monday mornings for coffee and monthly get-togethers at the club."

"Like last night?"

Davenport nodded.

Jake continued. "What is the name of the group? Do they have some way they identify each other?"

Davenport licked his lips and then said, "I think they call themselves, you know, 'Seek-and-Make'."

"That's quite a name, very suggestive. You a member?"

Davenport sucked in a cheek. "This is getting invasive. Do I need a lawyer?"

Jake saying now, "Up to you. By the way, who hired the stripper?"

"I don't know and that's the truth." As if the rest wasn't.

"You always were an enterprising guy, Jimmy, you know, the kind who wants to climb the ladder. C'mon you're a businessman, you have contacts and somehow you knew I was back from Texas."

"Yeah, I did know that, and you know who told me you were back?" Davenport smiled broadly, and said, "It was Harper Bannister. Yeah, Morgan, I'm seeing her, sorry about that, old sport. You know, though, Rhonda's available. Maybe you can take a shot at sloppy seconds."

Well, that would certainly explain Harper's reticence and why she wasn't returning his calls. Good work, Officer Morgan, another mystery solved but he didn't feel better for the knowledge. Jake found it odd that Davenport still held a grudge over Rhonda and now threw Harper at him as an insult. Jake stared at Davenport for a long moment.

"Thanks for the colorful language," Jake said. "Did your etiquette progression stall out in middle school?"

Davenport gave him a wolfish smile and then said, "Harper is a fine little piece."

That set Jake's teeth on edge, telling himself, 'poise, Morgan, poise'. Knocking Davenport out of his chair and stepping on his neck was appealing but he was, after all, a law enforcement officer and not a mob button man. Button men wore better clothes.

"You know, Jimmy," Jake said, rising from his seat, "you always were a tedious guy and it's too much work having to listen to you. Thanks for the information, though and we will talk again, and by then I'm hoping your memory will improve. Also, just between you and me, the next time you call Harper a 'little piece' I will slap the taste out of your mouth."

With that, Jake left the restaurant.

After Jake left, Jimmy Davenport made a phone call.

CHAPTER 5

Jake felt it was time to check out the community's leading source of information and that man was Leo "the Lion" Lyons, Paradise County's self-appointed historian, math teacher, and head coach of the Paradise Pirates High School Football team.

"Wait," said Leo, placing a hand to his forehead when Jake entered the football office, his antiquated D'artagnan mustache curling above his smile. "Lovesick dipshit returns to town, takes a pay cut, to comically chase after the always elusive female, who happens to be the daughter of his boss."

They were in Leo's office, trophies and team photos of all his teams of year's past, including last year's state finalist team. Leo was wearing a T-shirt with a Pirate logo, the pirate with a knife clinched in his teeth and a football in hand. Leo was the last guy you'd pick as a football coach, but he was one of the best and always the smartest man in the room, and if you didn't believe that he would be the first to tell you it was a fact.

"Just makes my day when I see you, Leo," Jake said. "You want to get off me and tell me what's going on with Harper."

"Last time you were here you were chased and seduced by your high school heart throb who took a shot at you and now you are doing the pursuing..."

"We're talking about Harper, Leo. Stay on task."

Leo looked up as if the answer were written on the ceiling fan. "Let's see, Harper Bannister, comely, intelligent, witty and smokin' hot daughter of your employer."

"I also work for Buddy."

"He doesn't have a daughter old enough for you?"

"You know I carry a loaded weapon, right?"

"If you shoot like you threw a football, I'll be safe. I do recall Harper and that she is too good for you, but I will try to help you. Harper has been on sabbatical, in Colorado for a week or two, but she's back now. Why didn't you just ask her dad?"

Because he didn't want Cal to know; he didn't want to involve Cal but he wasn't going to tell Leo that as the Lion would use the information to take another side trip.

"She's been seeing Jimmy Davenport." Jake shrugged, then made a show of looking at some of Leo's paraphernalia. "What I heard anyway."

Leo picked up a football and began spinning it in his hands. "My, my, I do love having an interesting ape like you around. Using your investigation skills to learn what she's been doing in your absence, yet you didn't know she was in Colorado. Jimmy Davenport? I don't know whether that's an upgrade." He looked Jake up and down, "Though almost anybody would be."

"Like I said, always good to see you, Leo."

"You need a dose of humility now and then." Big smile.

"I need some information on another thing, and you're always tuned in to the local rhythms. I have a list of names here." Jake produced the list and handed it to Leo. "Tell me about them. They call themselves 'Seek-and-Make'. I figured they were big names and hoped you could give me some background."

Leo looked at the list, then raised his eyes over the paper and shook his head. "So big I will have to pretend I don't know you for my own safety. Judge Carmichael? Dr. Thurgood? Colin Dukes? That's Dukes Industries, the biggest employer in Pinnacle County. Frank Jankowski, why he's...Whoa, here's one. Mickey Wheeler? This guy's a turd with legs and that's giving him credit. Why is Wheeler with these guys and why are you interested?" A look of recognition and Leo said, "Wait, this isn't about that dead girl, is it?"

Jake nodded.

Leo's hand slumped to his lap, the list still in hand. "Aw, Jake, you came back here for this? Okay, here it is, Judge Preston Carmichael is federal and well-thought of in this town and his father, Oliver Carmichael, is a king-maker who decides who gets what nomination in these parts; well, in fact the whole state. Thurgood is a shrink, keeps an office here two days a week, the rest of the time over in Medfield. He's a weird guy but has a large upscale clientele which means he knows what skeletons are in which closets and which wife or husband is on the hunt. People would not like him to start talking about anything. Jankowski? Loudmouth bully, but he's in the tall grass, one of the richest men in the area. His daughter was in one of my classes last year and we had an understanding about her behavior."

"What was that understanding?"

"That it was a long year and her whole job was to make sure I was happy every day. One of the perks of teaching a required algebra course."

"What about dad?"

"Like I said, he blusters and makes sure you know he's in the room. Big guy, hell of a football player in his day. He thought he could intimidate me about his daughter's grade, telling me I was picking on her." He closed his eyes, folded his hands on his chest and smiled blissfully. "A great moment. I told him he was right, I was picking on her, had it written right on my calendar. He sputtered around and I told him she would be treated equally bad-ly as anyone who didn't study and didn't complete her course work. We parted friends."

"Really?"

"No, he still dislikes me as there is no accounting for taste among the weak-minded. His wife, though? She's got the personality of a badger, without the positive qualities, but she is extra-deadly looking. Jankowski cheats on her but she doesn't care as long as her name is on the checking account , and he pays her Visa bill without question. Pretty sure she has a couple young boyfriends on the side. They're like the Addams Family."

Jake explained he was in the beginning stages of the investigation and asked which person would give him the most trouble on the list.

"Carmichael, of course, partly because of being a judge, but also because people like him. He gives generously to charity and his church and really is a good guy, though he is complex. Preston Carmichael has long been a community hero and is a fair judge who has helped many people in our community. He runs a charity auction every year for the high school. He is a bulwark and if he's involved; you'll be banging your head up against every hardcore Carmichael beneficiary in the county. The senator will run a close second. Jankowski will bluster and pose but he's hot air. Mickey Wheeler? A real shithook. I just can't figure him with the rest of those you mentioned. You're sure Mickey Wheeler was at the party?"

"He may be the man who brought in the dancer."

"The ex-dancer who has assumed room temperature."

Jake nodded. "Did you know her?"

"Yeah, had her in class a few years back, surprised she became a stripper. She was a messed-up kid, smart but another one of those young girls who looks in the mirror and sees a loser. I don't know if she's got much in the way of family. I never got a visit from anyone during parent-teacher conferences. In fact, I seem to remember she had a foster parent that didn't work out."

"You think of anything else and put your ear to the ground and let me know if you hear anything."

"I will do that and I'm glad I'm not you having to deal with these people," Leo said. "But then I'm always glad I'm not you as a settled disposition. I'll ask around."

"Do it subtly as I'm going to have to shake things up a bit and don't want you to catch any grief. Thanks, and congratulations on being a state finalist last year, I missed that."

"Finished second. Lost in O.T. Maybe this year we'll ring the bell."

"Second, huh? That's the first loser, right?"

"That's cheap, Jake." Leo chucked the football at Jake who caught it with one hand.

"Later, I'll buy you a drink at Hank's."

"I will allow it and probably will need two or three to assuage the hurt I feel from your disparaging and thoughtless comment."

"You've never felt hurt your entire life," Jake said, tossing the football back to his old friend.

"Well, there's that," Leo said. "One more thing, Jake, and I'm saying this as your friend, do not go at these people in your usual style."

"What's my usual style?"

"Balls-out, piss on the consequences. That won't work with these people, and they have the power to make trouble for you; a lot of trouble. Try subtle for a change."

"I do awesome subtle."

"Pretty to think so, isn't it?" Leo held up a hand and said, "One more thing, Jake, does it occur to you that perhaps 'Seek-and-Make' stands for 'S&M'?"

Jake had not made that connection, but he knew better than to compliment Leo on his insight as it would feed his ego.

"And now," Leo said. "You don't want to credit my withering acumen as you think it will give me the big head, but be at ease, Officer Lonely Hearts, my ego is self-sustaining."

This is why Jake made it a point to touch base with Leo the Lion periodically. The Lion knows.

CHAPTER 6

After his lunch with Jake Morgan, Jimmy Davenport made the call.

"This is Davenport. I had a law enforcement officer contact me today. You want to tell me what's going on?"

"What law enforcement officer?"

"Jake Morgan."

"Heard of him. I thought he went back to Texas."

"Here's an update, he's back and working for Paradise P.D. and asking about the stag party."

"He has no jurisdiction at the club. It's outside the city limits."

"He's cross-affiliated with Paradise County as an investigator. Working for both of them and he has homicide experience, but this isn't a homicide, is it?"

The man on the other end avoided the question. "What did he want to know?"

"He wanted a list of who was at the party?"

"Why did he want to know that?"

"The girl, Kandy Kane, the stripper? She's dead and Morgan says she was gang-banged."

Silence on the other end. "Well, don't panic."

"You know that I had...I wasn't the only one."

"More reason for you to keep your mouth shut. Besides, this is some small-town cop."

"You don't know Morgan like I do. He never stops.

Never. He'll eventually be around to visit you and we both know there's more to this than her death."

"What else did you tell him?"

Davenport hesitated. "Not much."

"What does 'not much' mean?"

"I told him about 'Seek-and-Make'. Just the club name, he already had a list of names."

"Why give the name of the club, asshole?"

"Had to give him something."

"You fucking swells give me a headache. Don't fuck this up, Davenport."

"I didn't do anything wrong. I just had sex with her."

"Who said anything was wrong, just that you shouldn't panic and turn it into something fucked up. But you fucked her and it would behoove you to avoid providing further information if there is anything to what this officer has told you. You realize that the police like to dangle half-truths and false information to get people to start talking about things they know or don't know? Keep that in mind, that is, keep your mouth shut and don't call me again."

Mickey Wheeler hung up on Davenport and Wheeler called another number with a fake name he had on his cell phone.

CHAPTER 7

Jake drove his late Father's restored Lincoln Mark IV into the parking lot of the Dinner Bell Café, a mom-and-pop landmark, located on what used to be the main drag before the influx of cash and influence blew up the small-town ambiance. Back in Jake's halcyon days the Dinner Bell was the main hang-out spot.

Jake saw Harper's new car, the little blue Ford Focus now replaced by a dark blue Jeep Wrangler. First thing Harper said to him as they got out of their vehicles was a remark.

"You seem familiar, do I know you?" Harper said, with raised eyebrows. Giving it to him about his lengthy absence.

"You look great," Jake said.

"Nice try, that won't work, Morgan."

"Thought I'd give it a shot. I call but you don't answer."

"It's like that Jimmy Buffett song, 'if the phone doesn't ring, it's me'."

Jake smiled to himself; she could get you going if you let her. "Look, I was gone longer than we talked about, but Texas transferred me to West Texas. That's a long way from here and sometimes a long way from cell service."

"You're going with that? That's your rationalization?"

"I'm doing my best. Can I buy your lunch and talk it over?"

She crossed her arms over her chest. "Someone else has already offered."

"Jimmy Davenport?"

She tilted her head to one side before she said, "Didn't take long for you to detect that, did it?"

"He told me, bragged about it actually, I wasn't checking on you."

"His ex-wife, Miss Paradise County, is available. Heard she and you used to be an item; there seems to be a throng of ladies around here who you used to be...a... intimate with, and probably a hit with the badge bunnies in Texas?"

"Where'd you hear 'badge bunnies'?"

"My dad is chief of police, I hear a lot of cop things."

"As for Rhonda that's in Davenport's head, I was never interested in Rhonda. She's nice but you heard incorrectly if you think I was some kind of Lothario."

"Lothario, huh? That's quite a thing for a guy who still wears Garanimals."

"They're easy to coordinate."

She turned serious. "What do you want from Jimmy? He said you were questioning him about an incident out at the Country Club."

"He said you told him about my homicide investigation."

"I'm the chief's daughter so I hear things. He doesn't have anything to do with any of that."

"I don't know that and neither do you unless you're his alibi. So, I guess my question is where you were Tuesday evening between the hours of six to one AM?"

He watched heat build in her eyes. Way to charm her, Morgan.

"You never learn, it's like you're vaccinated with stupid meds. If you want that to be your business maybe you should've made decisions that would've given you that right."

"I did and now I'm here."

"Dad told me you took his offer a month ago. Remember when you wanted to 'think about it' and needed a couple of weeks? Well, that was four months ago. How long did you think I'd wait?"

Jake nodded and said, "Fair question."

"Just a fair question? Is that what passes for an apology in your world? Did you see anyone while you were in Texas?"

"No." It was the truth. "I see it didn't stop you."

"You could've prevented that."

"You think Rhonda divorced Jimmy because it was selfish to keep him all to herself? First Tommy Mitchell and now Davenport. Maybe you should quit seeing assholes." Soon as the words left his lips, he knew it was a mistake.

She gave him the raised eyebrows again and looked up at him. "I do have quite a string going, don't I? I marry one asshole, seeing a divorced man now and in between a macho shithead who believes he can blow in like the wind and I'll run and jump into his arms."

"I want to see you."

"You don't want to see me, you just don't want someone else to see me. Write this down and memorize it; we make decisions based upon what we want rather than what we don't want. You disappear for months and then you are struck by an epiphany that you suddenly need to see me."

He looked away from her and then cut his eyes back to her. He shrugged.

"That's it?" she said.

"Well, I guess, I hope the best for you and Jimmy."

She met his eyes, her perfect teeth set in a straight line, and said, "You're exasperating. For a tough guy, you're kind of a moron, but I remind myself that you are hopeless regarding women. I told you once I had a crush on you since junior high."

"And now?"

"You give up too easy." She turned to enter the Dinner Bell and over her shoulder she said, "Think on it."

Okay, he would. Maybe not think of anything else.

***

Jake imagined cosmic wheels were determined to grind him down, and the thought was affirmed when the Mercedes-Benz rolled into the Dinner Bell parking lot and out stepped Rhonda Davenport. That Rhonda Davenport, Jimmy's ex. The Benz was sun-bright yellow, Rhonda liked people to notice her, and hard not to notice in the first place.

Rhonda was a willowy brunette with violet eyes and the assurance possessed by those born beautiful. Rhonda was lean, lithe and a tennis goddess. But to Jake she looked like dinner and a show in Manhattan when all he had were tickets to the circus.

"Well, look here," Rhonda said, her violet eyes bright, her orthodontist perfected teeth gleaming. "If it isn't the one and only Jake Morgan." She swept around the car as if the world were hers and said, "Come here and give us a hug."

She embraced Jake, her perfume was faint and alluring, and when they broke the embrace, Rhonda continued to hold Jake's shoulders in her hands, giving him the once over.

"You are still a handsome man, Jake. I missed you last time you were in town because I was on a cruise. When was that?"

Too long according to Harper.

"Good to see you, Rhonda. You look...well, incredible."

"Why thank you. I'm single again as I divorced Jimmy, the snake."

Looking for something to say, Jake went with, "Well, I'd say, local guys are in luck then."

She gave him a sidelong look, as if to decipher a hidden meaning before she said, "What brings you to Paradise?"

"I'm working with local law enforcement, kind of a free-lancer, you know, sweep the floors, wash the police cars, kinda thing."

"I doubt that," she said. "We should get together. I have this thing I have to go to. What are you doing tonight?"

"I have to work."

She gave him a sidelong look and said, "Are you

pushing me away, Jake Morgan?"

At the worst possible moment Harper walked out of the Dinner Bell with Jimmy Davenport at her side. Jimmy looked at Rhonda, Rhonda gave Jimmy the finger, and Harper gave Jake an expressive look and silently mimed the words, 'never interested' which Jake did not miss.

Strike two; Jake down in the count. Might as well swing for the fences.

"So what kind of thing is this tonight?" Jake said to Rhonda.

"It's a campaign fundraiser for Senator Stedman at the Country Club. You can mix it up with all the fat cats in a 100-mile radius."

Senator Stedman was one of the people at the club the night Cynthia Cross was killed.

"You know, Rhonda," Jake said, "I could use a night off. Eight O'clock work for you?"

CHAPTER 8

Jake drove to Dr. Zeke's office to see if he had any new information. Despite Zeke's rumpled attire, his office glowed hygienic.

Zeke told Jake, "She didn't die from being strangled. She died of asphyxiation, that is, he choked her slowly, perhaps as part of the sex act. I sent the forensic material on to the Highway Patrol, but I'll tell you, Jake, there was tearing in the vaginal tissue and also in the rectal tissue. She got worked over and she was pumped full of drugs."

Jake reached up and scratched at a cheek and grunted. "Job never gets easier. So, this was a gang rape?"

Zeke pursed his lips and said, "Yes, and well..." Zeke paused, allowing it to trail off as if that would make the horror disappear. "There's more."

"Yeah?"

"She's pregnant, DNA could determine the father for us if he's on file."

"And if he's not?"

"Then you'll have to dig some more. You and I both know the people at the party are big shots and there is the possibility none of the rapists have DNA on file."

Jake thanked Zeke and returned to the county vehicle. As he opened the door his police radio crackled, and the dispatcher informed him of a '10-99-J1 with a 'caution 3'.

From the code Jake knew this was an outstanding misdemeanor warrant and the 'caution 3' meant the person in question had either obstructed or perhaps assaulted an officer.

"Any clarification on the 'caution 3'?"

"You can handle it. Wait 'til you meet these guys," Dispatch told him. "This will be your comedy relief for the day." And then Dispatch gave Jake the location, which was Hank's Tavern, a local hang-out that Jake himself often frequented.

Upon arrival at the bar Jake found two men standing at the bar, with Hank the owner glaring at them with crossed arms and a short baseball bat.

Hank was his usual genial self. "What are you doing back in town, and what took you so long to get here?"

"Good to see you, too, Hank. What's the problem?"

One of the pair, a gaunt figure with a scraggly beard and badly faded jeans and an over-large Buffalo plaid shirt chimed it with his complaint, "I demand my rights as the town drunk."

"What right is that?" Jake asked.

Hank said, "He wants a magnum of Iron Horse Champagne which the idiot knows I don't carry."

"See that's a lie," declared the man. "I specifically requested Iron Horse Reserve Blanc de Blancs vintage 2016."

"You don't have the money for a shot of Thunderbird," Hank said. "How do

you even know what it is?"

"I have the money, oh yes, I do." Whereupon the man pulled out a wad of bills and fanned them in Jake's face. "See? You don't have Thunderbird, anyway, because I asked once and you said, no."

In the middle of a homicide investigation, he was dealing with eccentric drunks. Jake made a face and leaned away from the proffered money. "Okay, you have the money, but you don't have any right to obscure liquor orders. Could be wrong but you don't seem like a champagne kinda guy."

"That's judgmental," said the slender man.

Jake nodded. "I apologize."

"Dammit, Jake, get these assholes out of here," Hank said, his face a fist.

Jake held up a hand. "Okay, Hank, take it easy, I'll take care of it. You, Mr. Champagne, let's see some i.d."

"I demand to see my lawyer," the slender man said.

"I'm not arresting you, yet and it's not a request. Just give me your name."

"I will not," he said, indignantly. "I am a sovereign citizen and refuse to comply with this illegal detention."

Jake kneaded his forehead with a thumb and forefinger, thinking not this shit. "C'mon, not today, huh? I just want some i.d. and we'll go for a nice ride."

The second man, a smallish man wearing Carhart bib overalls and a pair of work boots chose that moment to take a swing at Jake. Jake easily leaned away from the roundhouse, caught the man by an overall strap, swung him in a half-circle and kicked his legs out from under him and then cuffed him in rodeo record time.

"I'm not responsible for him," the sovereign citizen said, pointing at his friend. "But thanks for coming to my aid, Little Sam. Hank, this place gets no more of my business."

"How will I go on, I'm fucking crushed," Hank said. "Do you see the kind of assholes I put up with, Morgan?"

Jake pulled Little Sam to his feet and said to Hank. "I've told you before, when you open up early, you get the squirrels." Then to the taller man, Jake said, "I'm going to have to confiscate that money you flashed." Jake held out a hand and flexed his fingers. "Hand it over."

"What? You can't do that?"

"Of course I can, I'm bigger than you and I'm the police. You're disturbing the peace and you have outstanding warrants, which is probable cause, and secondly if I run your sheet I'll bet you a magnum of Iron Horse Champagne there will be drug arrests in your history. Am I right?"

"I was framed."

"Yeah, they always are," Jake said. "You're under arrest for failing to appear, and I'm confiscating the money unless you produce evidence you legally obtained it."

Jake held out a hand and flexed his fingers, whereupon the man handed over the cash.

"I work. Part time."

"Doing what?"

"I...uh, do odd jobs. I sometimes get hired to clean up places."

Jake looked at the wad of money. "Odd jobs must pay better than I remember. Where?"

The man's eyes were furtive. "Well, I'm a substitute janitor at the school and sometimes clean up the American Legion building and the Country Club."

That got Jake's attention. "The Country Club? Did you happen to clean it up the night before last?"

"I refuse to answer as a sovereign citizen and on the grounds it might tend to incinerate me."

"It's incriminate, you ass, not 'incinerate'," Little Sam said. First words he'd spoken.

"Fuck you, Little."

Jake made a face; what a pair.

"Okay, are you going to give me your name and come along quietly or do I have to cuff you too? Either way we're headed downtown where I'll process you and we'll get –"

The man's eyes widened, and he bolted for the door with Jake after him. When the man reached the double doors, he bounced off the glass like a rubber ball and fell to the floor, leaving a spider web crack in the door.

"That's what you get, asshole," Hank said. "You're paying for that door, too."

Jake kneeled next to the man, rolled him over and cuffed him. The man had a cut in his forehead where he banged into the door. Jake cleaned up the wound, then asked the man if he was all right and helped him to his feet.

"His name is Rufus Crenshaw," Hank said.

Jake cut his eyes at Hank and gave him a look. "Thanks for your help, Hank. If you knew that, why didn't you say so?"

"You didn't ask me, you asked him."

Jake shook his head. "Wow, Hank, who knew you were a pain in the ass? One more thing, your doors aren't code. Get them fixed so they open out instead of in or I'll have the fire marshal here tomorrow."

Hank made a sour face and held his arms out. "Oh, so these two shitheads come in here, create a disturbance, but I'm the criminal."

Jake sighed and shook his head, thinking law enforcement work is so glamorous. Living the dream.

CHAPTER 9

Jake read the sheet to his detainee: "Rufus Crenshaw, 9-13-78, ht. 6-3, weight 160, priors: breaking and entering, trafficking controlled substance, public intoxication, public urination, indecent exposure, and resisting arrest." Jake paused to look at Rufus. "The misdemeanor warrants stem from a 'mistreatment of an animal' complaint where you shot at a neighbor's dog with a BB gun and a 'dash-and-dine' incident. You're a regular one-man crime wave, Rufus. Thinking about it though, what you really are is just a public nuisance."

"You don't have to be mean. I missed the dog, anyway, I think the sights are off on my BB gun."

Jake held up the wad of money he had confiscated from Rufus. "Who gave you this?"

"I saved up."

Jake shook his head slowly, held the money up and then said, "Yeah? Well, we've had some home invasions around town so I'm going to log it in as evidence unless you start telling me the truth about how you acquired it."

Rufus's mouth worked like a wounded bird, and he looked around the room and said, "Can I smoke?"

"Not unless you're on fire. Where did you get the money? I've got things to do, so be forthcoming or spend the night in county."

"They have good food there."

"Well chow down but kiss the money goodbye."

"What?" Rufus flailed his arms in the air. "I need...I mean, if I tell you can I keep it?"

Jake wanted Rufus to reveal the source without making promises he wasn't going to keep. Jake held up the wad of bills, letting Rufus see it, smiled, raised eyebrows and in a low voice said, "Well, I haven't logged it in yet."

"Okay," Rufus said, his eyes fixed on the money in Jake's hand. "Off the record?"

"Of course, we're friends, right?"

And Rufus told Jake the source. Jake's mouth almost fell open when he heard the name.

It was a name Jake knew was on the list yet still a surprise.

CHAPTER 10

Jake picked up Rhonda, at 7:30, and drove to the Country Club. Rhonda was dressed in designer jeans that were cuffed above her ankles, a simple dark blouse and sandals but she made them look like Givenchy designed them for her. When they walked into the lounge, Lanny Wannamaker shook his head. Jake helped her to a seat and then he walked to the bar and ordered Rye on the rocks for himself and a Pinot Grigio for Rhonda, a lady who made every male head turn and every woman glare at her man.

When Lanny handed Jake the drinks, he said, "She's way out of your league, Morgan."

"Sounds like envy, Lanny," Jake said, "And by the way, the other items I asked for I want before I leave tonight, or it's magic time in front of a judge."

"I've got your damn lists and receipts, just don't say where you got them," Lanny said. "Do you enjoy being an asshole?"

Jake put a dollar bill in Lanny's tip jar, winked and said, "How could I not enjoy it?"

The club was done up with bunting, a table of finger foods and an open bar. A pianist in a red tux was tapping out rock covers and oldies on a baby grand on a raised dais. There was a microphone set up for Senator Stedman.

Rhonda introduced Jake to people including Judge

Preston Carmichael and Dr. Drake Thurgood, both men were on Jake's list. Thurgood smiled and moved on quickly. Carmichael was younger than Jake would imagine, dressed in business casual, navy blazer with popover shirt, cotton pocket square, light tan khakis and brown tassel loafers. They shook hands and Carmichael raised his chin slightly to look at Jake.

"I hear good things about your Mr. Morgan," Carmichael said to Rhonda.

"I hear things about you also, Judge," Jake said, then hesitating a bit before adding, "Good things, too." Like why did you take my homicide victim's body?

Carmichael cut his eyes from Rhonda to Jake, without moving his head. He gave them a tight-lipped smile and said, "Enjoy the evening."

Jake held up his rocks glass. "This will be a start."

Jake and Rhonda mingled some more, Rhonda did more mingling than did Jake before they found a table and sat. They talked, playing catch-up, Rhonda was opening a dress boutique and was energized by the prospect, and was having her living room redone.

Frank Jankowski entered the room and sat down next to a young woman that Rhonda said was not his wife. Jankowski favored Rhonda with a curt nod.

"So, you know Jankowski?" Jake said.

"Yes, he owns a couple of housing developments east of town. He's one of my ex-husband's friends, also, thinks he's a player, and believes he received brood rights at birth. He hit on me once and I told him he made my skin crawl and to go home to his wife. Why do you ask?"

"The usual."

"Official?" she said.

Jake pointed at her wine glass and said, "Another one?"

Rhonda pursed her lips and said, "Not going to answer, are you, Mr. Inscrutable? It's okay, I understand, and yes, another would be nice."

Senator Wyck Stedman was introduced and made a few remarks thanking those who were in attendance.

This was getting interesting, Jake thought, if Mickey Wheeler and Jimmy Davenport could walk in now that's all Jake would want for Christmas. Get them all in one place and let them see him and maybe Jake might luck into a meeting of 'Seek-and-Make'. He was due for a break.

As if an answer to his inner question, five minutes later Harper walked into the lounge accompanied by Jimmy Davenport. Harper wore a loose-fitting shirt with elbow-length rolled sleeves over a lavender T-shirt, jeans and snow-white Converse all-star tennis shoes. Davenport saw Jake and Rhonda and glanced in the direction of the private room where Dr. Thurgood and the judge had gone. They ordered drinks and Harper pointed in Jake and Rhonda's direction and guided a reluctant Davenport to the table where they were seated.

Jake thinking, it just gets better and better.

Harper didn't miss a beat, pulling up a chair. Jake raised his chin and gave Harper a look. This was going to be good. One thing about Harper Bannister was that you didn't know what she was going to do next, but she was always going to do something.

"Hello, Harper. Jimmy." Jake said. "Have a seat."

"I already have one, thanks." She nodded at Rhonda who smiled back and swirled the wine in her glass. "So, what are you kids up to this evening?"

"Having a drink," Jake said. "Yourselves?"

"Jimmy's meeting some friends and I tagged along."

Jake grinned and said, "I think some of them are already here. Just waiting on Mickey though they already have a quorum."

Davenport looked like he had swallowed a quarter and took a swallow of his drink to wash it down.

"Who is Mickey?" Harper asked.

"Inside joke," Jake said.

"Speaking of inside jokes, I'm representing Rufus Crenshaw."

Jake shrugged. "Good luck with that and also with getting paid. That'll be a windfall for Jessup."

"It's pro bono," Harper said. "It's my understanding

you tricked Rufus into giving you information you needed on another case. What do you call tricking poor Rufus like that?"

Jake smiled over the cusp of his drink and said, "Top notch police work."

Harper gave him a look, then turned her attention to Rhonda and said, "I like your outfit, Rhonda." Meaning it.

"Yours too," Rhonda said, at ease. "Jimmy, you look like you're going to jump out of your skin. Are you coming down with something?"

"No. I'm fine. I...a...have to check on something." He rubbed the back of his neck. "I'll be right back." With that, Davenport stood and walked back to a private room.

"Where is he going?" Rhonda said.

"He has to check in with his meeting," Jake said. "It's a group of philanthropists, and community enhancement is their goal."

"You keep intimating rather than declaring, Jake," Harper said.

"Just trying to keep the conversation flowing," Jake said.

"Maybe you should quit trying to be ambiguous and come up with something intelligent and timely."

Rhonda leaned away and smiled enigmatically before she said, "I feel as if I'm caught in the middle of something. Do you two need to talk?"

"No, we're fine," Harper said, brightening. "Just filling in the dead air with old news. We used to be together."

"Oh," Rhonda said, brightening. "I know what that is, I was married to Jimmy and it's always something with these boys, no insult intended, Jake. Their idea of closure is hoping you're wasting away, clutching his photo and weeping."

The two women laughed.

Jake held out a hand, palm up. "I'm sitting right here," Jake said, amused by the conversation.

"Even better," Harper said.

"Yes, it is, isn't it?" Rhonda said.

"What the hell is Morgan doing here with your ex-wife?" Frank Jankowski asked Davenport. Jankowski gestured at Davenport with his rocks glass and some of it sloshed out in Davenport's direction.

"I'm not married to her anymore, Frank. She does what she pleases."

"Always did, what I hear," Jankowski said.

"Fuck you, Frank."

"Probably what Morgan will do to your wife."

Davenport never liked Jankowski and remembered when Rhonda told him that Jankowski had tried to pick her up. Jankowski used his size and his financial clout to intimidate people, and Davenport, while not immune to that, figured he had ascended enough where he did not have to take shit from the developer.

"Ex-wife, idiot. Try to remember that."

"Getting ballsy, huh Jimmy?"

"Shut up, Frank," Judge Carmichael said, on his third drink and his eyes were sleepy with alcohol. "We have more important things to discuss, though Mr. Morgan's presence, while intrusive, is probably a coincidence as Rhonda has always been a friend to the senator and would not bring 'ants to a picnic'. Let's address the issue at hand and then get back to the party."

On the ride home, Harper said to Jimmy, "What was your meeting about, if you don't mind me asking?"

"Usual stuff," Davenport said, looking straight ahead.

She turned in her seat and looked at the side of his face. "You seemed to jump quickly when your friends showed up. Didn't last very long, did it? Why was that?"

Rather than answering, Davenport said, "Why did you drag me over to the table with Rhonda and Jake?"

"Seating was limited."

"You had to know that it would be uncomfortable for me."

"Are you not over Rhonda yet?" Smiling to herself when she said it.

"That's not what I meant and you know it." Davenport

pondered her angle, the radio and the hum of the tires on pavement the only sound before he said, "You wanted to sit with them, knowing that would be awkward, now what was that little move supposed to accomplish?"

"What is wrong with sitting with people we know? I know Jake and you definitely know Rhonda."

"When you're with me I'll choose where we sit."

Harper laughed. "That's the way you think this relationship is going? I do what you tell me, Mr. Man? You're funny."

"Where is this relationship going?" Davenport said. "And what about you and Morgan? I know you used to be an item."

"Used to be?" Harper said it ambiguously. She had turned in her seat, so she was looking directly at his profile. She could swear he was grinding his teeth.

CHAPTER 11

Harper and Davenport left soon after Judge Carmichael and Jankowski. The judge waved to Rhonda but studiously avoided looking in Jake's direction. Curious.

Rhonda's elbows were on the table, she rested her chin on the back of a wrist. She said, "Jake, what's going on with you and Harper?"

"Nothing."

Rhonda shook her head and smiled. "Jake Morgan, you're still in love with her, aren't you?"

"Yet I'm here with you."

"Physically, anyway. It's okay, I understand these things. Jake, we're friends but you're no use to me if you still love her."

"Thanks, Rhonda. Always liked you."

"Oh, you're so full of shit," Rhonda said. She smiled her Miss Paradise County smile and said, "She's still in love with you, don't you see it?"

Jake took a sip of his drink and said, "Yeah, well, I don't see evidence of that."

"That's because you're a guy. Women do things differently. My guess is you did something or didn't do something, and you have to do your time in the barrel."

"May I ask you a personal question, Rhonda?"

"Seems we're already doing that, so go ahead."

"I've known Jimmy for a long time and we weren't

great friends, but I liked him. He's done well for himself, and he always had a thing for you, so what happened?"

"Why did I divorce him?"

Jake nodded.

"Well, when we were first married, it was a happy time, then Jimmy's father died, and Jimmy started making money...a lot of money. He seemed to think that's what I wanted. He would work long hours, and when I complained about our lack of time together, he told me, 'I'm doing it all for you, babe', which was not the truth. Jimmy wanted to be a big shot, a high roller. He stopped hanging around with his old friends and began hanging around with people I didn't care for."

"Like Frank Jankowski."

"Yes." She tapped a finger on her wine glass and then said, "And some women around town whose names I won't mention. Jimmy never liked Frank Jankowski in the first place, less so when I told him about Frank trying to get over on me. Is Jimmy involved with that murder thing?"

"Can't say."

"You mean 'won't say'."

"That too."

Rhonda was quiet, considering Jake. Rhonda was the kind of person always at ease and confident. "Jake," she said, "turnabout is fair play so may I ask you a personal question?"

He nodded and looked out the top of his eyes and said, "Sure."

"You never really had any interest in me, did you?" she said. "Not then and not now."

Jake looked at her, smiled and said, "You really look great tonight."

***

Police Chief Cal Bannister sipped coffee and said to his daughter, Harper, "You seem out of sorts this morning, darling. Why is that?"

They were seated in Cal's office. Harper wore a smart

blue business suit, as she had been interviewing her client, Rufus Crenshaw, and Cal wore his dark blue police chief's shirt and dark blue tie and was filling the bowl on his pipe.

"Officer Morgan railroaded Rufus into giving him information, making promises he didn't intend to keep." Then low, to herself, "Something he's good at."

Cal smiled when she referred to Jake as 'Officer Morgan', and then he said, "Oh, so it's about him."

"Why wouldn't it be? Rufus is my client."

"Are we talking about the same person?"

"Don't be obscure, Dad. We both know what *you're* talking about."

"Good, I want to be on the same page and what Jake, excuse me, 'Officer Morgan' did was elicit information in a homicide investigation. It's a lead and Jake has the type of homicide experience most small-town departments do not have and cannot afford."

"He misled Rufus."

"Yes, he did and that's good police work and there is nothing wrong or illegal about what Jake did. Look, hon, you're in love with Jake and now you're mad at him, so why not holster your guns and patch things up?"

"Who said I was in love with the jerk?" Cal smiled some more, and Harper said, "Don't smile at me like that. You don't know everything, you know?"

"Can't you at least sit down and talk to him?"

"Getting Jake Morgan to talk about anything is like pulling teeth with plastic tweezers. It's as if he was vaccinated by black-and-white cowboy movies. I talk about it, and he gets clever or makes short responses designed to allow him to walk around the subject."

"He's a little laconic," Cal said.

"He's stubborn and assuming about our relationship."

"*He's* stubborn?"

She made a face at him. "I saw him last night at Senator Stedman's fundraiser; he was with Rhonda Davenport, smirking away about how he had tricked Rufus."

"'Smirking away' huh? And who were you with?"

"You know I was with Jimmy."

"Oh, yes," Cal said, hiding his smile behind his coffee cup. "Wasn't he married to Rhonda at one time? So, I guess they're divorced now, right?"

"There's no way he gets off this easy."

"'He', meaning Jake? Does he know that?"

She smiled at her father and touched his shoulder. "He will."

***

Jake had places to go, such as Cynthia Cross' home or apartment, and people to interview, but Deputy Bailey told him she was having difficulty locating a known address. Dr. Zeke's receptionist called and told Jake the M.E. wanted him to drop by his office ASAP.

When Jake arrived, Dr. Zeke was agitated. The first thing he said to Jake was, "They took her."

"They took her? Took who?"

Zeke nodded. "How many dead bodies do you think I have?"

"Who're 'they' and why did you let them take her? She's evidence in a homicide case. How do you not have the ability to hold on to a body; it's like dealing with a rental car company? Did someone come in who needed a dead stripper body and she was your last one? Couldn't you have palmed off a Jane Doe?"

"Don't be an asshole. They had a writ to release her, and two court appointed officers picked her up. There was nothing I could do."

Jake placed his hands on hips, one hand resting against his service weapon. "Do we know anything about the body before they took her?"

"I did get DNA samples and maybe there is more I may have been able to glean from the body but, what I have is both interesting and vexing because so far, there is no DNA on file that matches the samples."

"Samples?"

"There were multiple DNA traces. Semen, scraping under her fingernails, saliva and it appears there were multiple rapists as you thought."

"Who signed the writ?"

"You'll never guess."

"Judge Preston Carmichael."

Dr. Zeke flinched, surprised. "Wow, how did you know that?"

"I'm a really good guesser."

"And yet still an asshole."

"Still that."

***

Rufus Crenshaw's information was on the mark. Judge Preston Carmichael was federal and worse, his father, Oliver Carmichael, was a former state senator, as well as a multimillionaire and a self-appointed kingmaker who had forced through nomination of U.S. congressmen and senators. Though his record at getting his people elected was spotty over the past decade, Oliver remained a formidable man as was his son.

Getting to Judge Preston Carmichael was not going to be easy and it did not make Sheriff Buddy Johnson happy when he heard Jake wanted to interview the judge as a person of interest.

"You'd better be damned sure of your information," Buddy said, as he brushed away Danish pastry crumbs from his shirt that dotted the upper part of his six-and-a-half-foot body. Buddy had been an all-state offensive lineman for the Paradise Pirates back in the day when Jake was the quarterback. "The Carmichaels can reach out and crush us both before breakfast."

"There any donuts around or did you eat them all again?" Jake said, looking around the break room. "And don't deny it, the evidence is all over your shirt."

"Dammit, Jake, this shit's serious."

"Never said it wasn't. You think you could leave me one donut hole at least."

"Where is your information coming from?"

Jake told him about Judge Carmichael's removal of the body and also the source of his information.

"Rufus Crenshaw?" Buddy winced and shook his head.

"Rufus Crenshaw is your source; are you trying to kill me? Crenshaw's the town character. You're going to make me a one-term sheriff, no doubt about it."

"Right off, I knew you'd like it. So, I guess I'll set up something with the judge."

"No," Buddy said. "That's going to fall to me."

"Are you pulling rank on me, Buddy?"

"Yes I am. Carmichael's a friend and more likely to talk to me. Who else is on your list?"

"You don't want to know."

Buddy absently dusted invisible pastry crumbs off his shirt and said, "I was afraid of that, but go through it anyway."

CHAPTER 12

Jake's first stop after leaving the Sheriff's department was to the county courthouse to see the Prosecuting Attorney, Darcy Hillman. Her receptionist informed Jake that P.A. Hillman was in conference with a defense attorney, but she would inform her that he was here.

Jake sat in the outer office and went through his list of names. Frank Jankowski, real estate developer; State Senator Norris 'Wyck' Stedman; Dr. Carmichael; Dr. Drake Thurgood, a psychiatrist; Colin Dukes; Mickey Wheeler; and a few others he could eliminate; some who had left early. Of course, there was still Lanny Wannamaker and Jimmy Davenport.

Jake knew Jimmy would be a weak link if there was a conspiracy due the fact that Jimmy was a lifelong 'wannabe', that is, somebody who aspired to be one of the cool kids but always fell short. Jake, growing up a farm kid with an alcoholic father and invalid mother, was never part of that group nor did he aspire to it. Jake concentrated on athletics, had a degree of success at it, and small towns have a way of leveling the class structure as you didn't want to cold shoulder someone whose shoulders you were going to brush against on a daily basis.

Judge Carmichael and Senator Stedman would be the toughest to approach and Jake was okay with Buddy talking to the judge for now, but eventually Jake knew he would have to tackle that one – not that he didn't trust Buddy; he did and always would – rather because Buddy would have to walk softly, and Jake would take the judge over the hurdles without Buddy's worries. Lanny Wannamaker and Rufus Crenshaw had been paid off, and even if Jake could get them to testify, their testimony would be easily impeachable at the hands of a high-powered attorney.

The outlier on the list was Mickey Wheeler, a Pinnacle County Kingpin who had been hauled in on DUIs, assault and there was a robbery charge years ago which was dismissed, ironically by Judge Preston Carmichael, file it away. Mickey controlled or managed strip joints in neighboring counties and was thought to be 'connected' to the KC mob. 'Connected' meaning he worked with them and kicked money upstairs but was not a finished wise guy. The question being now why was Mickey, a criminal, included?

The door to the prosecutor's office opened and Darcy Hillman emerged along with Charles Langley of Langley, Pope & Hardy. Langley was a high-speed attorney, a genuine heavy hitter, with whom Jake had some history.

"Young Mr. Morgan," Langley said, extending a hand. Langley was wearing a wool windowpane sports coat with dark grey slacks and a silk tie. Over his arm was a herringbone topcoat which cost more than a mortgage payment. Langley walked like a man going places.

Jake accepted the offered hand and nodded. "Langley."

"I thought you had returned to Texas after that unfortunate situation last year. What brings you here?"

"Business. And yourself?"

"The same."

"You may as well tell me now," Jake said. "Because I'll know as soon as I talk to Darcy."

Langley opened his mouth showing perfect bleached and capped teeth, then sighed. "I had forgotten your impertinence."

Jake smiled and said, "I thought my impertinence was legendary. I'm hearing your name a lot lately; some people I want information from are throwing you at me like you were a deadly weapon. Why is that?"

"What do you want, Morgan?"

"I'd like to interview the people you represent and I'm going to want some DNA samples."

"We'll see. DNA samples? Perhaps the clients you mention, yet have not named, had nothing to do with your investigation."

"Then the DNA samples will clear them. How about it?"

Langley ignored Jake, turned his attention to the prosecutor. "Well, then, Darcy," Langley said. "Always good to see you, and please give some consideration to our discussion and we will speak again."

After he left, they entered the P.A.'s office and sat. Darcy shook her head and said, "Why do you do that? You make my job harder when you aggravate an attorney like Langley."

"I need to ask you why my homicide victim's body was impounded, and my source tells me it was on Judge Carmichael's order."

Darcy Hillman chewed the inside of her cheek. "You are a lot of trouble."

"What I hear, too. Was it Carmichael?"

"I don't have the authority to divulge that..."

"I already know it was Carmichael, just checking to see if you had anything to do with it."

"I did not."

"Doesn't Carmichael's interest strike you as inappropriate or suggest ulterior motives?"

"Why would Preston have any untoward motives involving your homicide investigation?"

Calls him 'Preston'. Jake filed it away; though he knew Darcy Hillman was a straight-shooter and a fearless prosecutor, still, the lawyer fraternity was tight knit and would often circle the wagons when threatened. He would have to be careful as he threaded the connections.

Jake said, "Because he was at the Country Club the night that Cynthia Cross, who goes by the stage name Kandy Kane when she dances naked, was murdered."

Darcy reached up and rubbed the back of her neck. "You're kidding?"

"No, I am not." Jake read off the list of the revelers at the party and then handed the list to her.

Darcy framed her chin and cheek with a hand. She looked at the list and groaned. "This is not good and you're obviously here to inform me where this is going, and you will be requesting warrants. Now, listen, Jake, there are political realities and I'm not talking about a two-tiered way I will approach this, but the fallout is potentially radioactive for you...and for me. Therefore, I'm asking that you be extremely, and I emphasize, extremely sure of your information before you proceed."

"You ever hear of a group that calls itself 'Seek-and-Make'?"

Darcy sat back in her chair. "Why, yes. When I was in law school there was such a group. They were made up of students whose family were rich, well-connected and highly educated and was a sort of an offshoot of Yale's 'Skull and Bones'. Their fraternal members were very guarded about their initiation rites which were rumored to be satanic and sexually degrading, and if you bucked them, you were ostracized and attacked, and these attacks came mostly from the law school elite and even some outside the university. They were rumored to have held 'pig parties' where they had contests to see who could bring in the ugliest date, which was highly degrading and humiliating to the poor young ladies, and there were worse things."

Jake waited and then nodded at Darcy. "What types of things?"

"Well," Darcy said, then looked around the room as if there were apparitions listening in. "The Seek-and-Make thing? It was said, never proven, that the group abducted young women, gang-raped and then discarded them."

Jake said, "My homicide victim may have been gang-banged."

Darcy Hillman was a tough lady, but she put a hand to her mouth and said, "No, we can't have that. How did you come upon this?"

Jake shared what Dr. Zeke had learned so far and his interviews with Lanny Wannamaker and Jimmy Davenport.

"And now the body's been confiscated," Jake said.

"You think it's to prevent further forensic examination?"

"I will if you will."

Darcy tapped a finger on her chin, chewing on the information. "This is big and as I said, this thing is a landmine; a career-wrecking investigation."

"If they're willing to kill and cover, it could be more than just our careers at stake. I will tread lightly where I can."

"And a wrecking ball when you can't? Right?"

Jake nodded. "In the immortal words of Gary Cooper, 'yep'. Right now, I need subpoenas for DNA samples."

Darcy looked at the list of names, screwed up her face and said, "I heard you say that but what judge do you imagine will grant me subpoenas for Preston Carmichael? Or? Shit." She made a face. "Wyck Stedman? Have you lost your mind, you are genuinely asking for the moon and stars?"

"That's why you're my hero, Darcy. I have the utmost confidence in you."

"Drop dead, Jake."

"Yes, ma'am. Right after you get those subpoenas."

As he stepped outside the prosecutor's office, Jake ran into Harper, who was carrying a leather attaché case.

Harper greeted Jake with, "'Fancy meeting you here', would seem trite or overly formal so I'll just say, why're you here?"

"I could ask the same question," Jake said.

"I'm here to talk with Darcy about a court case."

"Rufus Crenshaw?"

She looked at him for a moment. "Maybe. "

"Just wondering, I didn't know a paralegal could argue in court."

"You've been gone too long, I'm ready to take the Bar exam."

"It was good to see you last night. Too bad Jimmy had to rush off to his meeting. Just ran over there like a little puppy dog, didn't he?"

"So, how're you and Rhonda making out?"

"We're friends."

"Yes, well the same for Jimmy and I?"

"Did you tell him that?" Big smile. "Love to hear his reaction."

Harper shook her head and then looked off to one side then back to Jake, and said, "It didn't come up. I suppose you told Rhonda you were just friends?"

"I did."

Her eyes widened merrily. "I forgot how blunt you can be. Jake, what are we doing here? You don't do small talk."

"I heard small talk was the new sexy, so I've been working on it."

"No, intelligent discussion is the new sexy, so that leaves you outside again."

"So, do you want to go have coffee and small talk?"

She looked at her watch and said, "I have things to do. You know, Jake, you were gone for months, way past your due date and now you wonder why things aren't swinging your direction. Did you imagine while you were off chasing coyotes in Texas that I was sitting by a candle-lit window, waiting for my prince to ride up my driveway?"

"I kind of like that image, let's go with that."

She set her perfect teeth in a line and said, "You are the reigning champion for saying the wrong thing." She brushed by him without a word or a look.

"Good work, stupid," Jake said to himself. "You crushed that one."

CHAPTER 13

Jake did some homework on his list and all of the men in question had attended Missouri University. Checked online and also did some background on Cynthia Cross. No known relatives, which meant her name might be as fake as her stage name, and Jake hoped Bailey could scare up some relatives. He made a mental note to check on a birth certificate that matched the date on Cross' driver's license. It might mean nothing, but you never knew what might be significant.

One of the names on the list was Frank Jankowski, who was a 40-something land-developer, like Rhonda had said, who had bought low during a real estate downturn and then sold large during the boom years. Jankowski had been a local football hero back when Jake was in grade school, and was recruited by several Division I schools, before he popped his Achilles tendon at a fraternity party his freshman year.

Jankowski's home was a rambling two story with a three-car garage and a football-sized lawn. When Jake rang the bell, a slouching teenaged girl with ripped jeans and a nose ring answered the door. Jake remembered what Leo the Lion had shared about the girl.

"Oh," the girl said. "I thought you were Conner, but as usual the dumbass is late. What do you want?"

Money, power, and an ocean view condo, but he kept

it to himself, so instead Jake introduced himself as the Paradise County Investigator and said he was there to speak with her father.

She made a face. "They're around back in the sunroom." Then she shut the door.

Smiling to himself, Jake said, "A wonderful young person."

The sunroom was more like a hybrid rec room/sunroom, with a large deck that led to a tarp-covered swimming pool and a dressing room at one end. Jake was met at the entryway by a beautiful dark-haired woman with an impassive face.

Jake introduced himself and the woman said, "I know who you are. I'm Felicia, Frank will be down momentarily."

Felicia and Frank, the alliteration couple.

"Do we know each other?" Jake said. "I've been away —"

"My maiden name was Kellogg. You put my cousin in prison."

Great. "She put herself there."

"After you fucked her, right?"

Her cousin would be Pam Kellogg Mitchell who, yes, Jake had arrested for the murder of her father-in-law. Pam had also been Jake's high school sweetheart and first love.

"So," Felicia said. "Are you here to arrest Frank or just fuck me?"

Her warmth and charm certainly explained the daughter, Jake thinking, man, the people you meet. Best part of the job.

Jake raised his chin and arched his eyebrows. He motioned with a thumb over his shoulder and said, "I'll...a... just wait outside on the deck."

"Suit yourself." Felicia Jankowski gave him a dismissive look and went to sit at a low table in the covered section of the room and dismissed him as if Jake were invisible. So, they were not going to be best friends, after all. Among officers there was a law enforcement saying that 'after three years on the job you don't make any new friends, only new enemies' and that was at work here.

While Jake waited, he scanned the area of the upscale neighborhood which was huge gabled homes with sprawling yards and swimming pools.

Frank was talking into a cell phone that looked like a domino is his over-sized paw. Frank was telling someone, "I don't care what your thoughts are, do what I tell you. Goodbye." He pocketed the cell then to Jake said, "It's a hell of a thing you just show up. Why didn't you call?"

Jake raised his eyes and said, "I have better luck when I don't announce my visits." Jankowski was a big man, with a face like a hatchet, and a beef-and-bourbon face, heavier than Buddy Johnson and Buddy was six-foot-six and tipped the scales at 265.

"Who told you I was here?"

"Your daughter," Jake said. "Lovely girl."

Frank gave him a narrow look, deciding whether or not he was being insulted.

"I heard about the chippy," Frank said. "I don't know anything about her."

"What chippy?" Jake said. "I'm collecting for the heart fund."

"Heard you were a fucking smartass, but you know the one I'm talking about. You know I was at the party, but I left early."

Everybody leaves early, thought Jake, it was like an epidemic or an agreed upon dodge.

"When was that?"

"About eleven."

"Can anyone verify that?"

"My wife, Felicia."

"You won't mind if I ask her?"

"Go ahead."

"I will, she's a real talker, your wife. Who told you about the stripper and what did they say?"

"Again, I don't have to say anything to you."

"Okay, I can get a subpoena and you will talk to me, and we'll do it at my office or, you know, in court with a judge. How about volunteering a DNA sample? That'll clear you."

"I know about you," Jankowski said, snorting. "You imagine you're a hard case, think you're cute the way you come at people."

"Who told you about the dead girl and what did they say?"

"It's all over town, on the news...what difference does it make? Look, I contributed to Buddy Johnson's campaign, and maybe I'll talk to him."

"I'll tell him you're a big fan and he can count on your vote. I still want to know about what went on that night at the party. Who hired the dancer? Did you know her before?"

Jankowski looked over the top of Jake's head and then back at his wife. "Let's do this by the pool."

They moved to a poolside sectional couch with one of those large umbrellas that was suspended by a hook-shaped pole. Next to the sectional was a large cooler which Jankowski opened and produced a can of Budweiser, slick with icy wetness, which he proffered to Jake.

"You want something to drink?"

"No, I'm good."

Jankowski reached into a shirt pocket and produced a pack of Marlboro Light cigarettes and shook one loose and said, "No, I didn't know the girl and don't know who hired her. I don't need that; I've seen naked women before. Lots of them."

"So, you must be one of those studs I hear so much about." Remembering what Rhonda said about Jankowski's reputation as a skirt chaser.

"I get tail and it's none of your business."

"But you want me to know about it, anyway, and you know, it could become my business. You know Mickey Wheeler? You might know him as 'Mickey Wheels'."

Jankowski bent over his cigarette, fired it up with a disposable lighter, and while looking down said, "No."

Jankowski had a tell, what some investigators called a pantomime, that is, something a person did when they were lying or not wishing to communicate the truth. Jankowski was an egoist, which made him overconfident.

"I ask because Wheeler was at the club party the night in question."

Jankowski drew on his cigarette and looked over Jake's head at something on the horizon as if Jake wasn't there. "Oh well, he must be that guy I didn't know. What about him?"

"He gets around, like the flu, he infects things."

"Well, I don't know him, okay?"

"Did you have sex with the stripper?" Might as well see where it goes.

"The fuck you talking about? Man, I don't fuck whores, and you just wore out your welcome."

"She was a whore? Let me write that down so I don't forget; is that why she was hired? So, again, how about a DNA swab?"

"You got any more questions you can talk to my lawyer."

"Be glad to, I may know him; who's your lawyer?"

"Charles Langley."

What a small world.

"All right then, we're done here," Jake said. "I'll talk to you and Langley at another time, until then, don't run off and join the circus or anything."

"Anybody ever tell you, you're an asshole?"

"It's been said." Jake left him with his big house, his bored wife and bitch-in-training daughter.

CHAPTER 14

Jake Morgan's first impression of Dr. Drake Thurgood, College Professor and licensed psychiatrist, was that Thurgood was a man who smoked a pipe as a prop, gestured with it when he spoke and also as a guy who missed the hippie movement by twenty years. When Jake asked questions, the good doctor gave Jake sleepy-eyed looks over the top of his glasses when he spoke. He also didn't strike Jake as the type to strangle and beat a young stripper to death, but Thurgood had been at the Country Club and from experience, Jake knew you couldn't judge killers and rapists by appearance.

"One of your patients was a young woman named Cynthia Cross, correct?" Jake said.

"They're 'clients', not 'patients' and I am not at liberty to divulge personal information about my clients."

"She's not going to object as she's dead and I already know you were seeing her. She was an exotic dancer and it's interesting that someone like that was seeking treatment."

Dr. Thurgood gave Jake a studied look over his rimless glasses before he said, "All types of people seek therapy. Being an exotic dancer, as you say, could be a reason she sought treatment or has nothing to do with why she saw me."

Jake smiled to himself, knowing Thurgood had unwittingly admitted to treating Cynthia Cross.

"Well, I have you on a list of names at the Country Club, the night she was performing there. Tell me what you know about that night."

Thurgood's mouth fell open and then he nipped at the left side of his mouth with a tooth. "I was not there. It would be a breach of ethics for me –"

"I already know you were there," Jake said, cutting him off, wanting to keep Thurgood off balance, turning the tables on the therapist who would be used to asking questions rather than answering them. No one willingly admits they were present at a crime or in this case, at the Country Club, meaning they know things they won't say. "Nothing good going on that night and you knew her and that connects you. So, you were at a party where one of your clients was the main attraction. I don't know, it's just me, but it seems like a breach of ethics. What do you think?"

Thurgood's mouth worked. "I already told you I was not there when she arrived."

"No, you said you weren't there, so help me here, I'm trying to get my head around how you know when she arrived if you weren't in attendance?"

Dr. Thurgood shook his head quickly and said, "Well, I heard about her...a...terrible thing and I should have chosen my words more carefully."

"When did you show up and when did you leave?"

Thurgood made a show of examining his pipe as if it contained his answers. He stirred the ashes with a pipe tool and some of the ash fell to his lap, which he ignored.

"I was at the club earlier. I had tennis lessons with the club pro."

"I will check on that, but I have a witness who tells me you were at the club party the night the young lady was doing the shimmy-shake in her undies. Can you account for your time from nine to one in the morning on the date in question?"

"Yes, of course. I was home."

Nobody wants to admit they were there, yet nobody

has a reliable alibi. Further, no one seems particularly concerned that Jake was asking questions.

"Are you familiar with a fraternal group called 'Seek-and-Make'?"

Thurgood hesitated before saying, "Why, no I haven't."

"But you did attend Missouri University."

"Where are you going with this?" Thurgood said. "Do I need to employ a lawyer? I don't know about such things and yes, this is a tragedy that young Miss Kane was killed, but I believe I need to consult with an attorney before continuing."

"That is your right," Jake said, thinking it was time to brush the good doctor back from the plate. Jake stood and thanked Thurgood for his time, telling him he would contact him if he had further questions. As Jake was walking to the door, he turned and said, "You know, I always wondered, do psychiatrists ever cure anyone?"

Thurgood seemed surprised by the question. "No, it is not like curing a cold, but we help them learn to cope."

"See?" Jake said. "That's the difference between us because cops cure sick individuals. We put them in prison."

Take that, Dr. Cool Pipe. But Jake had his doubts about the shrink as a killer, but Thurgood knew more than he wanted to reveal.

***

Sheriff Buddy Johnson called Jake and said, "How's it going? Are you learning anything?"

"I've never had it so good," Jake said. "So far, I've learned nothing, have no leads, nobody was there, nobody did anything wrong, case closed. How did it go with the judge?"

"I made an appointment to meet with him later today."

"I'll go with you."

"No, that's the last thing I want."

"I just want to go and observe your investigatory style."

"And not say a word?"

Jake lifted a hand as if swearing-in. "Cross my heart and hope to die. I'll be very diplomatic."

"You don't have any practice at diplomacy and you're not going."

Jake broke the connection and rang up Cal Bannister, telling him he was coming by the office.

Cal and Jake sat in the break room of Paradise P.D. Cal offered Jake a cigarette which Jake declined. "Good for you," Cal said. "Breaking the habit."

"It was nothing," Jake said. "I've hardly thought about a cigarette since I quit three days, two hours and twenty-three, no twenty-four minutes ago. I've got problems with the Cynthia Cross case, and it is going to cross both county and city jurisdiction."

"Not a problem, that's why Buddy and I share you."

"Buddy is going up to talk to Judge Carmichael about why he was at the Country Club the night Cynthia was killed."

"Are you talking about Preston Carmichael?" Cal gave a low whistle. "You're in the big leagues there, boy, better hitch up your pants and don't get your chin out over the plate."

Jake nodded. "Good advice. What I think is happening is that I'm going to get squeezed and information withheld. Carmichael issued a writ to remove Cynthia's body."

Cal leaned away and squinted at Jake. "You're kidding?"

"Wish I was."

Cal was quiet for a long moment before saying, "Jake, this is going to get very nasty, very quickly, so where do you go from here?"

"I've got to keep pushing. I'm going to talk to Mickey Wheeler and a couple other guys who were at the club. Deputy Bailey interviewed a couple of other party goers and said she had something for us, one of them a guy named Adam Driver."

"Good," Cal said. "Getting somewhere.

"Bailey will interview the family, if she can find them."

Bailey had informed Jake that she was having difficulty running down an address for the murder victim, telling him that there was no Cynthia Cross nor Kandy Kane in Medfield or anywhere in the area, meaning she was using yet another alias. "I've got a couple other deputies checking with some other people who were in attendance. Thing is, no one will admit they know anything about the girl or were there, even though I have witnesses to the fact they were. There is a murder and a gang rape, and nobody really seems all that concerned about my investigation."

"And you're worried you're not getting anywhere?"

"No, I'm concerned they don't realize what a badass I am. I have a reputation to consider. I'm trying to get DNA samples either volunteered or by subpoena."

"Good luck with that," Cal said. "If you get a subpoena for that group, I want you to buy my next lottery ticket. The last thing this bunch will want known is that they get their jollies watching naked girls writhe around."

"'Writhe around', huh?" Jake said. "That's pretty good."

"You like that? Word gets around, people like the judge and Dr. Thurgood are into such things; it could hurt their standing and they are all about their standing."

"Jankowski let me know he has sex with multiple women and women are hell-bent clawing at his zipper to get at it, but he wasn't interested in the stripper."

"Sounds like him, though he is unlikable, he's not stupid."

"Thing is, how do I reconcile people like a judge, a senator, a big time businessman like Colin Dukes and Dr. Thurgood who are concerned about their image with a jerk like Jankowski and worse, a dirtbag like Mickey Wheeler? This is a very eclectic group of suspects, but they're also a member of some frat boy club called 'Seek-and-Make' which may or may not be a euphemism for 'S&M'. I want to know how that strikes you."

Cal pursed his lips and nodded. "Could be there is more to this than just the homicide. You have a bunch of people from different backgrounds engaged in inappropriate behavior and now you throw Mickey Wheeler, a known criminal, into the mix and I smell extortion."

"I considered that, but who is being blackmailed? Jankowski could give a damn what anyone thinks other than he has the fastest zipper in town, and none of this hurts Wheeler, it's even a resume enhancer. That leaves the senator and Dr. Thurgood."

"And Judge Carmichael, who removed the body."

"I'm wondering if these guys have done this before or have just graduated to this level. Maybe they've just teased at it before and now they need more stimulation to jack up their libido, the kind of thing serial killers evolve to."

Cal drummed his fingers on his desk and said, "We've had rare homicides, but any murder combined with rape I've encountered has been by one man, either an ex-boy-friend or some other individual, so gang rape is a new one for me. Are you having any other problems?"

"Just your daughter."

"So I heard," Cal said. "You gotta remember, Jake, her mother ran off and left us when my Harper-girl was small. She's bound to have trust issues because of that and you kind of disappeared on her for months."

"I realize why she's mad, that's my fault, and I under-stand abandonment issues, but how about you, you don't mind my asking, how were you able to deal with it?"

"I had a tough time when Elizabeth left us, very hard times, but that was twenty years ago, and I had Harper and I knew she was watching so I hid it deep. It takes a while, but time does heal such things and I'm doing fine now."

"She's dating Jimmy Davenport and treats me like I'm radioactive."

Cal smiled big, rubbed the back of his neck and said, "She's punishing you a little bit, dangling Davenport in front of you. That's my daughter."

"You should've raised her better," Jake said.

"If I had, she wouldn't be interested in a lowlife like you."

"Well, that hurts," Jake said. "Give me one of your cigarettes."

"I thought you quit."

"And I did," Jake said, reaching to accept the proffered cigarette from Cal, "for three days and 29 minutes."

CHAPTER 15

Sheriff Buddy Johnson's interview with Judge Preston Carmichael hadn't gone well.

"He was cordial at first, even magnanimous," Buddy said. "But when I pressed him for details, he became oblique, and he is effective at word games. He is highly intelligent and let me know without saying it that he had the ability to reach out and touch both of us, in particular, you."

Buddy and Jake were sitting at their favorite corner table of Hank's place. It was late evening, they had long-neck Coors in front of them and were waiting for Leo the Lion to join them.

Buddy continued, saying, "He mentioned you would be "more effective" if you conducted your investigations with more sensitivity."

"So, word is getting back to him. I touched base with his friends which means they're talking. What was his story?"

"Said he wasn't there."

"Of course he wasn't." Jake shook his head. "Nobody else was there so why should he be the only one in attendance. If I didn't know better, I'd think these men are being surreptitious."

Buddy snorted and took a sip of his beer. "And they have a sharp legal mind like the judge to help them over the hurdles, not to mention another equally adept attorney in Charles Langley. I asked him about his writ to remove the body of Cynthia Cross from our M.E. and his take was there was another case with a 'civil rights' violation involving Cross."

Jake leaned forward and made a face. "What? What the hell is he talking about?"

"It's bullshit of course, but he's federal, and I don't know how to get around him at the present. Jake, you kicked over a basket of snakes here. The most sinister thing he said was a threat about people who had their careers ruined."

"Meaning you and me?"

"He didn't mention us, just told me a rambling story about a couple of investigators he knew that never worked again, but I didn't miss the implication. And yet, he treated me with the utmost respect and propriety."

"'Propriety' huh? Did you ask him about the 'Seek-and-Make' club?"

"He never heard of it, of course."

"How about a DNA sample?"

"We didn't get around to that."

Leo the Lion entered the bar and hollered at Hank to bring him a beer, but as was the tradition between Leo and Hank, the beer was already on the way. "Quit your damn yellin'," Hank said. "I ain't one of your football players."

Leo sat and said, "So how's the investigation going?"

"Fantastic," Jake said. "Haven't learned a thing and nobody knows anything. I could give a clinic on how not to conduct an investigation, but mostly, I blame Buddy here."

Buddy jammed a thumb in Jake's direction. "It's because I hired this guy can't open his mouth without pissing people off."

"Well, when you have a gift," Leo said. "You go with it. Buddy, has our friend, the expatriate Texan shared his latest romantic predicament?"

"Why no, he has not," Buddy said, with a delighted look. He leaned forward and said, "Tell me more."

"His one true love, the fair princess, Harper Bannister, is giving him the wind due his ass-backward courting style, wherein he proceeds with his usual pattern of ineffectiveness, because he is useless, but he can't help it, as that is who he is."

Jake sipped his beer, leaned back in his chair and considered his friends. "I'm so happy I'm a source of amusement for you married guys. Why don't you get a dog or something?"

"Harper's too good for you anyway," Buddy said.

"You're right," Jake said. "That's why I'm here medicating my regret with the two sorriest people I know. Anyway, she's dating Jimmy Davenport."

"You're kidding," Buddy said. "He's part of our investigation."

Jake nodded. "Correct, therefore I have to be careful or she'll think I'm hanging him out for personal reasons."

"You want me to assign someone else to interview Davenport?"

"No, I'll stay on him. I think he has more information, and he won't be as tough to break down as some of these others. Did your deputies learn anything from canvassing the area where we found her?"

Buddy shook his head. "Not much. I assigned Makepeace and Johnson to some of the people at the club but like the rest, they didn't learn much except that Cynthia Cross worked at a juice bar in Medfield, one of those stripper joints, called 'The Gentleman's Club'."

"I'll check that out," Jake said. "We're not getting anywhere quickly. What is it they always say on those television cop shows, 'the first 48 hours are critical'? Well, we're past that."

Buddy gave him a look. "There are people on your list that can drive a shit train through this investigation."

Jake nodded. "Dr. Zeke gave me the results of the DNA samples today. There were three different profiles, none of them on CODIS so we have perps who have never committed a criminal offense or at least haven't been caught."

"In English, without the acronyms," Leo said. "What is CODIS?"

"Combined DNA index system," Buddy said, clarifying. "We send samples off to the FBI in cases like this one and then the computer matches on file. We can't take samples of every arrest, some people we arrest are exempt from providing samples like minors under seventeen."

That was when Harper and her friend, Sherry Hammersmith walked into Hank's, and Jake's throat tightened up.

"Speak of an angel and in she walks," Leo said, paraphrasing the idiom, and then he quoted Lord Byron, "She walks in beauty, like the night of cloudless climes and starry skies..."

"...and all that's best of dark and night meet in her aspect and her eyes," Jake said, finishing.

Leo gave him a look and said, "My, my, you're not always the stupid hick, are you?"

***

First thing Harper did after entering Hank's place was to peripherally search out the corner table where Jake often sat with Buddy and Coach Lyon. There he was.

"There's your ex," Sherry Hammersmith said. "Do you want to leave?"

"Calm down, Sherry, this is fine."

They sat and Hank brought over a Chardonnay for Harper and asked Sherry what she would like.

"I'll have a Chardonnay, also, Hank," Sherry said.

"Take this one," Harper said, sliding the wine glass in front of Sherry. "Double Jack Daniel's with a splash."

Hank gave her a funny look, then walked away to fulfill her order.

"Double Jack?" Sherry said, casting her eyes at the corner table. "Well, here we go."

"Don't read anything into it. I had a rough day at work billing clients, which are few and Jerry's clients, which are many. That and one of my clients is a petty thief who is not helping me."

Sherry sipped her wine, and said, "He is cute, isn't he?"

"The petty thief?"

Sherry wrinkled her nose and smiled at her friend. "You know who I'm talking about."

Harper shook her head and said, "Drink your wine, Sherry."

"Touchy, touchy. We're sensitive today, aren't we? And I don't believe a word you're saying."

"Okay," Harper said, "it's not really a good time between us. He has tried some, but Jake is what some call reticent, and my dad calls laconic. In his own way, Jake is wanting to heal this thing up, but I can't allow him to disappear for months at a time and then slip back into town and all's forgiven."

"Of course," Sherry said, and covered her mouth. "Why that would be...too easy and then you wouldn't have an excuse to drink hard liquor."

Harper tilted her head and said, "I can feel your smile, Sherry. Yes, he's cute and yes, I still have feelings for him, but..."

"But what?"

Harper blew air through her lips. "I just...you knew my mom ran off when I was five and never came back?"

Sherry nodded. "Yeah, sorry about that."

"Well, fortunately, I have the best Dad in the world, but he had to work long hours as a police officer before he became chief, but even a little kid like I was knew how hard that time was for Dad. There are things about Jake that are like Dad but there are also some things that are, I don't know..."

"Maybe like your mother?"

"I remember her and knew she loved me and that's what I didn't understand and don't understand. How do you run away from someone who claims to love you?"

"And Jake loves you?"

Harper nodded. "Says he does but there is a part of him that is distant and there is a kind of resentment which he tries to tamp down and keep to himself. Both of us had difficult relationships with our parents. Jake and his father fought all the time due to his father's drinking and emotional abuse of his mother. Jake loved his mother and she died while he was in high school, leaving Jake and his dad to pick at each other. Jake took off for Texas after high school and didn't come back for ten years. Jake didn't attend his father's funeral."

"But didn't Jake's father leave him the house and the farm?"

"Yes, and it appears Jake has settled into a type of 'separate peace', if you don't mind the cliché, concerning his late father."

"Didn't you tell me the other day that he had just been promoted by the Texas Rangers?"

Harper nodded.

Sherry put a finger to her lips and looked at Harper for a long moment.

"What, Sherry?"

Sherry shrugged and then said, "So, he gave up a prestigious position in a well-regarded organization to come back to little old Paradise. Seems like he gave up a lot to come back to a place he really didn't like and no motivation. Now, why would he do that?"

"Don't read anything into it," Harper said, and took a good swallow of Bourbon. "Jake Morgan will always surprise you."

CHAPTER 16

Mickey Wheeler operated out of a hangar-sized car repair garage in Medfield in Pinnacle County. Before leaving Paradise, Jake checked Mickey's record – several old assault charges from Wheeler's youth, some B&Es also from that time – racketeering, vice, narcotics, and a homicide beef he had walked on, but few convictions except for those from his teen years, most of which had been expunged.

Mickey Wheeler had learned some things.

"Don't take him lightly, Jake," Buddy said. "The guy is slicker than hair oil and keeps some real dirtheads around, they're like a gang. Let me send Makepeace with you."

"I was a Texas Ranger," Jake said, ramming a fresh magazine into his SIG Sauer. "And there's only one gang."

Jake arrived in his late father's restored Lincoln Mark IV, a regal black two-door that rolled down the highway like a cloud. When he got out of the car, a man in greasy coveralls offered to buy the Lincoln.

"Man, that's a sweet ride, bro," said the man. "What you take for it?" The man made 'what you' sound like whatchoo.

"Not for sale," Jake said. "Mickey around?"

"Inside. Office in the rear. Who are you?"

"Nobody."

"I smell cop."

"You see a badge?" Jake said.

"Just the same, I need to clear this with Mickey."

Jake waited and could hear the man's half of the conversation.

"Guy here wants to see you." Short pause. He looked at Jake. "What's your name?"

"Jake Morgan."

"Says he's Jake Morgan." Short pause, and then the man cut his eyes at Jake. "Knew it, you're a cop."

"You'd clean up on Jeopardy," Jake said. "Am I going in or not?"

"Yeah, go ahead, but I knew it."

Inside, Jake's nostrils filled with the heavy odor of oil, grease and dirt. There were two vehicle hoists, one with a late model Camaro on it, wall racks of tools and engine parts strewn about which suggested that Wheeler's garage was doubling as a chop shop. Further suggestion of that possibility were three guys standing around smoking cigarettes, looking tough and drinking beer. Wheeler wasn't worried or he wouldn't let Jake inside which meant either Wheeler was paying someone off or blackmailing people at the courthouse.

"What kind of cop are you?" one of the men said. "You don't have a uniform or a badge."

"I'm undercover," Jake said. "I disguise myself as a mechanic and infiltrate chop shops."

The three men laughed. "Go on in."

Nothing better than criminal types with a sense of humor, Jake thought.

When he entered the office, Mickey Wheeler was on the phone, a cigarette smoldered in a large ashtray in the shape of a brake caliper. Wheeler was a smallish man, under 5-10, with a Harvey Keitel nose, and bushy wolfish eyebrows. Wheeler pointed at a chair and Jake sat.

"Just get it here," Wheeler said to his phone. "If you can't do that for me, then that's a different conversation, so do you want to have that one? Good, we agree you don't. Thank you." Then he hung up.

Wheeler put his forearms on the table, revealing jailhouse tattoos on his left arm, most likely self-drawn.

"Been expecting you," Wheeler said. "Figured you or the Spook."

"You thought Caspar the Ghost was going to show up?"

"No, the Jig sheriff." Big smile on Wheeler's face, testing Jake's patience.

"Interesting ashtray," Jake said.

"It's a conversation piece."

"People come in here and talk to you? That amazes me. Are they mostly masochists? Or just stupid people?"

Wheeler leaned back and smiled some more. "Heard you were a comedian, so we're not going to get along, right?"

"Up to you," Jake said. "My job's the same regardless of whether I find you entertaining or not. You know a young woman named Cynthia Cross?"

Shaking his head. "Never heard of her."

"She also goes by the working girl name, Kandy Kane, actually works at one of your clubs. Funny you don't know about her, you must have a large workforce of women who dance naked. Somebody killed her and left her in a ditch on a dirt road after they beat her up. Of all the guys at the Country Club the last night she was alive, none of them fit the 'beat the shit out of a woman' type. You're the closest to that."

"You don't know me but you're going to insult me, right? That some new form of interrogation you boys learned down in Texas?"

"This is my subtle, wait until you see me pissed off."

Wheeler laughed and looked at Jake some more. "This is going to be fun."

"Not for both of us, and not eventually."

"I don't see a badge."

"I have one but you already know who I am and couldn't wait to show me what an informed guy you are and knew I was a Ranger, but I got other things to do. You were at the Country Club the night Cynthia Cross was killed, no use denying it, and probably lined up the dancer. What I can't figure out is how you fit in with the Country Club crowd, not that you're not an upscale guy, but rather that you didn't graduate college."

"You think a guy has to go to college to be a success? That hurts."

"No, but you have to be a college grad to be a member of their little group. They ever mention "Seek-and-Make" to you?"

Mock surprise from Wheeler. "No, they did not but it sounds a bit like 'grab and fuck'."

"Some," Jake said, "More like rape and murder or S&M. Just wondering if you're in the rape and murder business or just vice and protection?"

Wheeler raised his eyebrows. "You." He shook a finger at Jake. "You are something new and I'm going to have to watch you very closely. You're not the typical cop I run into most days. You're thought-provoking, I will need to be more careful and as a friendly nod, you should also be careful."

"Why would that be? Because of you?"

Wheeler threw his hands. "Oh, no, I'm a fuzzy teddy bear. There're other people you don't know who will take a nasty interest in you."

"What if they take a nasty interest in you?" Jake said. "If you know something, what makes you believe you'll be safe from retribution?"

Wheeler smiled, slid open a drawer and produced a Kimber Colt .45 semi-auto. He held it and then slowly laid it on his desk, purposely pointed at Jake.

"Well, I've got this," Wheeler said.

"Nice piece," Jake said. "Kimber .45. The rumor around the campfire is that you killed two men."

"I heard that, too, but I didn't use this."

Jake produced his own sidearm, a SIG Sauer and held it out for show and said, "I prefer mine. SIG Sauer, it was my service pistol."

Wheeler rubbed his face and considered Jake as if suddenly seeing him for the first time. "That's a .357, right? You expecting Water Buffalo?"

"No, just assholes."

"You don't know if mine's loaded or not?"

"I don't care, as we're getting along." He leveled his eyes with Wheeler's eyes. "This one is loaded; it's always loaded and it's always with me."

"Yes, we are getting along, aren't we?" Wheeler placed the weapon back in his drawer. "I like you."

"As a token of our new friendship," Jake said, and winked, "give me a couple names."

Wheeler raised his arms and did jazz hands. "No. No, I don't do those things. That is a heads-up and by the way, from now on you talk to my lawyer and his name is –."

"Charles Langley," Jake said, finishing it for him.

Nodding his head now, Wheeler smiled in appreciation and said, "Wow, sharp, I do really kinda like you. But don't count on me for help, I'm just a poor garage owner trying to get by."

"Yeah, I saw some of your mechanics outside. I didn't know that leather sport coats and Italian shoes were the new look for grease monkeys."

Wheeler tossed a hand in the air. "Those guys? They're my consultants. By the way, this isn't your jurisdiction, is it?"

"This is a homicide investigation, so I get to run around everywhere for information."

"You were an investigator in Texas, right?"

Jake nodded. "Yep. Keep that in mind next time I visit with you and your attorney."

"You ever need some body work, I'm your man; we fix up dents and broken pieces better than anyone in town, even give you a discount. You have a good day, Officer. You know the way out, right?"

"Yep." Jake stood, started to walk away then paused at the office door, turned and said, "Next time I see you with a gun in your hand it'd better be smoking or made of chocolate because I'll make you eat it."

CHAPTER 17

"Mickey Wheeler is not the killer," Jake said to Sheriff Buddy Johnson. "But that doesn't mean he isn't an accessory."

"How you figure?" Buddy said.

Buddy's office was as clean and organized just as Buddy was as an individual. Wall photos were arranged symmetrically, and Jake would put money that Buddy used a level and a tape measure on all of them. The papers on the walnut desktop were orderly and squared to the dark leather desk pad blotter. Buddy's shirt was creased, and his tie was knotted in a perfect Windsor. Jake's friends were a study in contrasts. Where Buddy, a physically imposing man, was immaculate and orderly in his life was a contrast to Football Coach, Leo the Lion, who was a semi-slob whose office was strewn with papers and coffee mugs stained with extended use. In school Buddy worked hard to make the honor roll and Leo was the valedictorian with little effort. Leo was as close to a genius as Jake had ever known.

"Wheeler's not worried even though his DNA will be on file due his criminal record," Jake said. "He's smart, very smart and will know we ran DNA profiles."

"But the body was removed."

"Yeah, that's bizarre, but Zeke kept semen samples, so the body was removed for a different reason. No,

Wheeler knows or has an idea who killed her and may even know who or how many assaulted her, but he didn't. He's too smart for that. He's a career criminal, flourishing in the Barton County seat and operating pretty openly. I wouldn't doubt he is a member of the Chamber of Commerce and the Rotary club. I talked to him, and the guy can hold his own with anybody. Wheeler is not very concerned about his position in the criminal hierarchy in Medfield and I think that's because he pays off the right people, and those he can't buy he blackmails and because his game is blackmail, my guess is that is what is going on here with our homicide case."

"You think he set up the murder?"

"No, I think he brought in the stripper and the gang-bang, whereas the homicide was an unintended consequence that works out even better than he'd hoped. There is just something here that doesn't fit, but I haven't figured out what it is."

"You think he has a big fish on the line?" Buddy said.

Jake nodded. "There were several at the party and Wheeler will have no qualms about milking the situation."

"Wheeler must have nuts the size of softballs to do this. Anything else?"

"He's James Dean cool," Jake said. "You ate all the doughnuts again, didn't you?"

"Forget the doughnuts, Jake."

"Sure, Boss."

"And don't call me, Boss."

"How about Cookie Monster?"

"Get the hell outta my office, do some work, and shut up."

"No hug?"

***

One of Wheeler's men, a guy named Richie, stepped into Wheeler's office and said, "Everything cool, Wheels?"

Wheeler tumbled an opened pack of cigarettes on his desk with his hand, turning it over and over, thinking about things. "You know, sometimes you run into something that's a real dead ringer for something you ain't never seen before."

"The cop?"

Wheeler nodded. "We need to keep an eye on him. See what you can do; also I need to know about the bartender, Lanny 'Someshit', wait, Lanny Wannamaker and also the janitor are doing. See if they're spending time with my buddy, the Texas Ranger."

"What Texas Ranger?"

"Yeah? Good question?"

***

Before leaving the office, Jake made sure to touch base with Bailey. Deputy Sheriff Bailey while not a woman of action, she was a solid law enforcement officer who possessed a C.J. degree and was comfortable with internet and computer technology. Add to that, she had a nose for and a doggedness for detail that Jake admired. Jake needed to know more about 'Seek-and-Make' and he hoped Bailey could research that.

"I'll be glad to do that," Bailey said. "What things do you want to know?"

Jake sipped coffee from a paper cup and said, "Initiation rites would be a starting point and that will be tough because they're supposed to be a secret ritual. I don't know much about it but you might start with research into Yale's "Skull and Bones" as this S&M thing is supposedly an off-shoot."

"S&M?" Bailey said. "You making that connection?"

"No, actually someone suggested it to me."

"Well, I heard of it when I was in college," Bailey said. She rummaged through a box of pastry. "Have you noticed we're always out of doughnuts?"

"I've got a suspect, a physical description, and I'm closing in as he leaves a trail of crumbs."

Bailey saying now, "I remember 'Seek-and-Make' as a bunch of Greek Geeks, you know, Frat boys, whose rich parents paved their future with contacts and money."

"Why, Bailey, I may have to turn you over to the

Fraternity anti-defamation league. I already have it on good authority that several of our partiers were members. Check the backgrounds of these people." He handed her the list of his suspects. "See if they were all members of the same fraternity and years of graduation and who they hung out with. Maybe some of their old college buddies can give us more information."

"I'll take care of it."

"I have every confidence you will," Jake said.

Bailey smiled and when she left Jake decided that Deputy Bailey was a valuable resource who had been overlooked in the past.

Jake knew his next step would be Senator Stedman and that would be a tough knot to unravel, but he figured the politician had more to gain through cooperation than by resistance. If he cooperated fully, then Jake might be able to mark him off his list, and if he didn't?

Well, Jake had something for that, too.

Jake dialed up P.A. Darcy Hillman on his office phone and asked about the DNA subpoenas.

"Resistance," Darcy said. "I told you this wasn't going to happen. No judge wants to subpoena Preston and the senator. How are you doing with getting them to volunteer?"

'Preston' again.

"The same. They throw Charles Langley at me like he was a grenade."

"He is. Be careful."

Jake drove to the state capitol to interview State Senator Norris "Wyck" Stedman. After Jake survived the buffer zone of aides, consultants and a too-smiley receptionist, "Wyck" Stedman, was gracious but cautious as Stedman was a leading candidate for U.S. senator. The good senator made a show of receiving Jake into his office.

Jake was offered coffee or water which he refused and shown to a seat, a nice leather wingback with the great seal of the state of Missouri, two bears standing over a circled buckler with a half moon and a federal symbol, stamped on the seat back. It had always struck Jake as weird that there were bears on the seal. Although there are a smattering of bears in Missouri, Jake, despite many hours hunting had never encountered one nor had anyone Jake knew.

Stedman dismissed his aide after Jake was seated and the façade dropped. Stedman wore a grey business suit with a crimson rep-tie. The senator's fingernails and hair-cut were perfect.

"What can I do to help you, Deputy Morgan?"

"Investigator." Jake said, correcting him, not because he wanted to show off his title but rather to throw Stedman off balance. One of Jake's interview tactics was to correct a suspect's behavior such as making them to sit up in their chair rather than slouch, thus establishing the relationship between law enforcement officer and person of interest. It worked even with people in high places like the senator.

"I'm sorry, Investigator Morgan," Stedman said. "I understand about the importance of titles, and I misspoke but please tell me the reason for your visit today? Is it official?"

"Senator, I know you keep well-informed, and you also appear to have the power to suppress information, which in this case, serves my purpose, as we have not released names of suspects in the homicide of a young lady named Cynthia Cross who you may know as exotic dancer, Kandy Kane."

Stedman concentrated on rearranging items on his desk. "I don't recall anyone by that name."

"Are you sure this is how you want to play this? Think hard on that one. I'm sure Preston Carmichael has already contacted you after he was interviewed by Sheriff Buddy Johnson. The Carmichaels, in particular, the judge's father, Oliver Carmichael are two of your biggest backers. I don't see them hesitating to dial you up."

The senator placed his elbows on his desk and pointed at Jake. "You are creating a problem for yourself here, young man. Careers are ruined by such things and..." pausing for effect, Stedman continued, "careers are made by utilizing opportunities if you appreciate what I'm saying."

"Senator, either you talk to me, or you talk to the grand jury when I've completed my investigation. Whether you are involved in the murder or rape, that's right, Miss Cross was raped and beaten, but it won't make any difference, you'll still have to talk to us at some point and the scandal will probably pole-axe your nomination for the U.S. Senate. The Carmichael's will not be able to bail you out of this one, as they can't stand the scandal to touch them."

Stedman glared at Jake for a long moment, staying with the intimidation tactic which Jake found amusing. Jake broke the silence and said, "So, do your damnedest and you can save the tough guy looks, I've looked down the guns on Mexican Cartel thugs and you're not a patch on them. So, tell me about the night at the Paradise Country Club."

"You can talk to my lawyer, son."

"I'm not your son and if you think throwing Charles Langley at me as a terror tactic, that's right, I know about Langley's web of clients here, you should understand that will not slow me down. Further, as I said, we have withheld names of suspects, but if you're going to talk through an attorney which is your right, then we may be moved to make a press release to increase the pressure."

"Are you threatening me?"

"No, sir, I am informing you. I realize you're used to sycophants and law school students but I'm neither. So, I will leave now to set up a time to interview you and lawyer Langley, and you will be there. As for Langley he knows me, and I can't wait to get his reaction for yet another opportunity to visit with me."

Stedman started to speak, changed his mind and looked down at his desk and then at the windows. He wiped his mouth with a hand and said, "All right, Jake, may I call you 'Jake'?"

"Why yes, sir, you can." Jake thinking, now we're getting somewhere. "How about a DNA sample?"

CHAPTER 19

Cynthia Cross, AKA: Kandy Kane, had previously worked as a pole dancer at "The Gentleman's Club", which was Mickey Wheeler's roadhouse in Pinnacle County outside Medfield.

The Gentleman's Club was a metal building, with a raw gravel parking lot; inside, the muted, multi-colored lighting created a surreal environment as if Jake had entered an alternative dimension. Jake cornered a "dancer" whose stage name was "Meryl Strip", real name Hillary Edson, who was one of Cynthia Cross' best friends. Hillary was unabashedly uninhibited by her body as she wore only a pair of high heels and a bikini bottom while talking to Jake.

"Yeah," Hillary said, "Cynthia was my friend, we hung out and even shared a place for a while before she got this fancy apartment at the Village Manor that some guy was paying for. I miss her."

"Did you know the guy?"

She shook her head. "No, saw him a couple times but she wouldn't tell me his name."

"Can you describe him?"

"It's dark in here, you know," she said.

"If I showed you some photos, do you think you could pick him out?"

"Well, maybe, hey, are you a cop?"

Jake shrugged. "Yeah, I hope that won't hurt our friendship."

"Our friendship?" She laughed. "You're cute, though. I hope you catch the guy who killed her. Does my outfit make you uncomfortable?"

"I've seen naked women before."

She opened her arms and said, "Well, you like what you see?"

"Yes, they're lovely but I need information about this man who paid for her apartment. Did he come in often and did you ever get a close-up look?"

"What a reaction. Why are all you decent guys such prudes?" She said, flirting with her look. "No, I never got a good look because when he came in, he had his own table near the back and the lights would be turned down. Besides, Mickey, that's my boss, he told us that the guy belonged to Cynthia only."

"You're telling me that Mickey Wheeler and this guy were friends."

"No, I wouldn't say that. It was like an arrangement, I don't think the guy liked Mickey that much, though I'd see Mickey laughing and chatting the guy up, but the guy himself never laughed. In fact, he never seemed happy to see Mickey."

A large man wearing a leather vest that would fit Godzilla walked over to them and said, "You, fella, what're you doing here? Meryl, you gotta get ready, you're on in fifteen."

Hillary made a show of crossing her arms under her breasts and smiled.

Jake swept a hand in her direction and said, "Looks like she's good to go."

"Who're you?"

"I'm a fan. Who're you?"

"I'm the guy decides who gets to stay."

"That's Cartwright, we call him 'Hoss'. And, Cartwright, hon, this is the heat." She looked at Jake and said, "Always wanted to say that, that okay?"

Jake nodded.

"We got special accommodations for cops," Cartwright said. "You really a cop?"

"Got a badge and a card with my name on it."

"Well, she's done talking. Get up, Meryl, and get busy unless this guy's gonna pay."

"I hate to pull rank on you, Hoss, but I'm not finished talking to her."

Hoss blinked, unsure now. "I don't know if I can allow that."

"Call Mickey," Jake said. "He gave me permission."

It confused the big man who pulled up a cell phone and then moved away from them to call Mickey.

"We'd better hurry," Jake said to Hillary. "One more question."

"You don't have permission from Mickey, do you?"

"Nope, don't need it, but better than wasting time with 'Hoss'. You think Mickey had something on the boyfriend."

Hillary leaned forward and stroked Jake's forearm before saying, "Baby, Mickey got something on everybody."

***

Jake left the club and drove to Village Manor Apartments on the West side of Medfield. Jake told the manager he was investigating the homicide of Cynthia Cross.

"I'm sorry, Officer," the manager, a young lady in a smart business suit whose brass nameplate identified her as 'Brooke Baker, Manager', "but we don't have anyone by that name staying here."

Jake said, "She was here under another name. You couldn't miss her; she would be the type of young lady that men look at and women wish they looked like." Jake produced a photo of Cynthia Cross and Ms. Baker's eyes widened.

"Oh my god." She quickly covered her mouth and colored. "Pardon me. That's Sylvia Crane."

"Have you seen her recently?"

"Why, no." Ms. Baker's eyes looked downward, "No, I haven't."

"I would like to see her apartment, if that's possible."

"That's unusual and we're not allowed to do that."

"I already have a warrant to search Cynthia Cross' home and I can easily get it amended if that will help but, Ms. Baker, Sylvia is Cynthia Cross and Cynthia Cross is dead.

"This is horrible."

"How was the apartment paid for? Did Miss Cross or Miss Crane pay for it by check? Did she pay in person?"

"Her rent was paid for two years in advance, and I remember that because it was so unusual."

"Who paid it?"

"It was paid in cash. I didn't take the money; one of my employees made the arrangements."

"I want to talk to that employee."

"He doesn't work here anymore."

"Where can I find him?"

"That won't be possible, Mr. Morgan. I'm afraid Mr. Philpott died yesterday."

CHAPTER 20

Harper Bannister ate lunch at her desk and listened to the police scanner as she did. She finally arranged bail for Rufus Crenshaw, having to pay out of her own pocket.

"That's not something we do," her boss, Jerry Jessup, told her. "You start paying for their bail, they will work you and then they will expect it, plus they might just take off on us."

She knew Jerry was right; she was annoyed at Jake and wanted to frustrate him by bailing Rufus out, but she knew there was no telling what Rufus would do once on his own again.

She didn't have long to wait to find out.

The police scanner crackled. "Two car accident on Highway 68 southbound, Highway Patrol on the scene, ambulance in route. White male, Rufus Crenshaw, 325 Maple, Paradise."

Harper got up and headed for the door.

***

Jake called Darcy Hillman to make sure he was Kosher going through Cynthia Cross' AKA Sylvia Crane's apartment on the original subpoena. Darcy told him she would amend the document but for now "go slow and let the wheels grind. You can police tape the domicile but let me make this clean so if you find anything we can use it when we prosecute".

Jake taped off the apartment and called the Medfield Daily News to check on the death of the apartment manager, Ralph Philpott, and learned that Philpott had drowned while fishing, which Jake found interesting. Jake asking the reporter if there was any notion of foul play, the reporter telling Jake the police dismissed it as an accidental drowning. Jake wanted photos of the people attending the Country Club party to show Hillary Edson, the stripper, when he got the call; wreck on State Highway 68 South.

Jake saddled up his county unit and arrived to find that Corporal Fred Ridley of the Missouri State Highway Patrol was already there along with an ambulance and a wrecker.

Ridley took one look at Jake and smiled. "I thought you Texas boys wore Stetsons and cowboy boots. You look like you buy your clothes at 'boring R us'."

Jake held a finger in the air and said, "Didn't I see a poster of you at a park with a shovel in your hand, talking about forest fires?"

Ridley offered his hand and Jake shook it. "Good to see you, Jake. What brings you back to Missouri?"

"I'm working."

Ridley looked at him, "As what?"

"Law enforcement."

"Who'd have you?"

"I wanted to be a trooper, but I passed an IQ test."

"Heard you were working for the sheriff as an investigator. Where's your badge?"

"It's at the cleaners. What have you got here?"

"High school kids who can't drive and a drunk who shouldn't. About ninety percent of every accident report, I can write either 'inexperienced driver fault or under the influence'. Guy blew point 0-six. Fortunately, the kids are not hurt badly, some cuts and bruises."

The kids' names weren't familiar but the name of the alcohol impaired driver was Rufus Crenshaw who was now yelling Jake's name.

"Morgan. Hey Morgan, it's me, Rufus."

"One of your friends?" Ridley said. "I should've figured on that."

"I had him inside, but somebody bailed him out."

"Marshal Morgan," Rufus said. "I need to talk to you."

Ridley raised his eyebrows and said, "Marshal Morgan?"

"He's the town character. You mind if I talk to him?"

"Go ahead."

Jake pulled Rufus aside. "Okay, Rufus," Jake said. "I'm not a marshal, I work for the sheriff and the city."

"So what do I call you?"

"Jake is fine. What is it you want to tell me?"

"I'm in a lot of trouble here, ain't I? This wasn't no accident because I was drinking, which I was, but the brakes didn't work."

"Well, you blew point 0-six, which will be a DUI, and knowing your history it doesn't look good."

Rufus looked around as if ghosts were lurking. "I have the information you want." He looked around some more and then in a low voice, said, "About the party at the Country Club."

"What is it?"

"Not here," Rufus said. "Can you get me off the driving impaired?"

Jake shook his head. "I don't think so; this is the Highway Patrol's party, I'm just here to assist, but I can talk to Trooper Ridley for you and maybe, if you're willing to testify—"

"Testify!"

"Yes, testify and if your information leads to a felony arrest, then we can probably get Darcy Hillman to reduce or even drop these charges. I'm not making a promise other than I will try, but I believe she will like it. But no more pissing in the street, annoying Hank or bothering the neighbor's dog."

"They're following me."

"Who is following you?"

"Not here."

Jake looked at Rufus for a long moment and said, "Let me talk to Trooper Ridley."

Jake shared what he had with Ridley.

"I'd heard about the girl, Cynthia Cross," Ridley said. "You think this guy has real information or is he trying to dodge the DUI?"

"Both," Jake said. "But I'd about piss on an electric fence to turn the key on whoever killed her. She was treated badly, and so far, things are going slow."

"Okay," Ridley said. "How about I process him at your station and lock him up there so you can question him about the other thing? I do this, just realize that my lieutenant would rather burn a drunk driver than have sex so I'll have to break dance to a Christmas song to get him to go along."

"I'd like to see that."

"I'll video it for you."

CHAPTER 21

Harper was held up by a phone call so by the time she arrived at the scene of the accident, only the wrecker with the name of the company 'Wilson Wrecker Service', stenciled on the door, was still on the accident scene. The driver of the rig, a black man with greying hair, was hooking up as she got out of her Jeep.

"Hello, Miss Harper," said the driver of the wrecker, a man she knew, Angus Wilson.

"Hello, Angus. Where is everybody?"

"A state trooper and Jake Morgan took Rufus Crenshaw to jail. His fault for the accident. The two kids went in the ambulance, but they looked fine."

"Jake Morgan was here?"

Angus smiled. "Sure was. You and Jake kinda had a thing once, didn't you?"

Harper thought, small towns never forget.

***

"So, the boss is eating my ass out about Hillary talking to the cop," Cartwright said.

"That's Meryl Strip, right?" said Cartwright's buddy, Richie. Richie was a gearhead, almost a genius with cars, who could drive anything with wheels, drank too much and was a recovering meth head, as much as those guys could recover, and like Cartwright, both men worked for Wheeler, though Cartwright worked as a bouncer at the Gentleman's Club and Richie worked at the garage fixing cars. Sometimes Mickey used Richie for collections and Richie was good at it.

"Yeah," Cartwright said. "That's her."

"It's confusing," Richie said. "How you keep up with all those fucking names? I mean, there's Meryl Strip and another called Birdy Bends and what's that fine one called, you know the one got dusted over there in Paradise County."

"Kandy Kane. Her real name was Cynthia something, anyway Mickey's all pissed off because some guy from Paradise County was talking to Hillary, I mean Meryl, whatever."

"Meryl Strip is that one with the mouth. She'll do a lap dance but touch her and holy shit, she goes full she-bitch. I'd like to hit that. So what's going on with Meryl baby and why did the cop want to talk to her?"

"She's Kandy's best buddy."

Richie whistled. "Law dog trying to make connections here. Why did you allow him to talk to her without talking to Mickey?"

"Cop said he had permission from Mickey, told me to check."

"Fucking cops lie. I know that guy you're talking about." Richie reached up to clean something from his teeth with a fingernail. "He was out there at the garage the other day."

"Man, why you gotta stick your fingers in your mouth? Go wash your hands."

"Wiped it off on my pants."

"That's another thing, Richie, you're a nasty motherfucker, always doing shit like that, when you got dirty fingernails from the garage. Shit, I can see the grease under your fingernails."

"Now you sound like those bitches at the club, whining about that shit. You work at a garage, you get that, and it's fucked up hearing you, a guy works in a bacteria trap like that strip joint, get all whiney about a little grime when you work in a place imports chlamydia and herpes like it was a cash crop. Anyway, so the boss is pissed about the cop, what his name? Wait, yeah Morgan that was his name."

Hoss said, "Got an attitude like he ain't some small-town cop."

"Boss says the guy was a Texas Ranger and not to underestimate him. Never heard Mickey talk that way about the police."

Hoss shook his head like a bull shaking off a fly. "Don't make no sense he's working for that Podunk County."

"Yeah, well, now we may have to do something with Hillary Meryl what's her ass."

"I like Meryl."

"Don't matter what you like, you whale looking mother-fucker, it only matters what Mickey wants."

"Watch your mouth, Richie. I want any shit out of you I'll squeeze your head until your ears meet, you stinkin' narrow-assed grease monkey."

"You'll always be what you are, Hoss, but I'm way more than a fucking grease monkey. You just aren't sharp enough to see it."

***

Trooper Fred Ridley brought Rufus into the Paradise County Sheriff's office and processed him through Paradise County's system whereupon the custody of Crenshaw was remanded over to Jake.

Jake removed Rufus to an interrogation room at the sheriff's office, which was basically three folding chairs and a state surplus table. Rufus once again asked if he could smoke, Jake forever amazed at the things he put up with.

"We talked about that before, and the answer hasn't changed. You are occupying a lot of my time and I didn't realize I had taken you in to raise. Now, I want to talk about the information you have regarding Cynthia Cross."

"Who?"

"Kandy Kane."

"Oh, you mean the stripper. Yeah, I got something you can use, but I want to know how you're going to protect me and how –."

The door burst open and Harper Bannister entered the room. "Neither one of you listens very well, I told you, Rufus, you don't talk to this man unless I'm present and you, Morgan, you know better."

Jake looked up at her and said, "All the interrogation rooms in all the towns in all the world and she walks into mine."

"You think this is funny?"

"I will if you will. Look, Harper, this isn't about the earlier arrest."

"I heard it on the scanner. He had a wreck and I –."

"This isn't about the DUI either," Jake said. "If you'll slow down, I'll explain, and I actually welcome your presence as he needs advice. He has information about a case I'm working on."

"I'm still not happy about tricking him into giving you the initial information and you will be careful about what –."

Jake held up a hand and said, "I want to find out what he knows. How do I get you to shut up without making you mad?"

"You can't, but..." she started to say more, shook her head and fought a growing smile. "You'll just do it again."

"You two know each other?" Rufus said.

"Vaguely," Harper said, looking at Jake.

"She's infatuated with me," Jake said.

"No, Rufus, we are not married. Officer Morgan thinks he is funny, and I am tolerating him."

"You ain't married or nothing, right?" Rufus said. "I mean you sound like married people."

Harper looked at Jake and then back at Rufus. "I'm smarter than that."

"My job is hazardous enough without that," Jake said. "Can we get back to why we're here? Rufus, I want to know what happened that night at the Country Club that you haven't told me before."

"You don't have to answer that, Rufus," Harper said.

Jake shook his head, then to himself said. "Where's my pepper spray when I need it?" He turned to her and said, "I thought we understood that he was going to make a statement and you're interrupting again."

"I'm advising him of his rights."

"You see a recorder anywhere? Anything he gives me is off the record for now, I just need a direction. He doesn't start talking, we'll go through on the DUI bust, which, added to his long list of petty crimes will land him in county for an extended time, and then we will ask these question anyway, without any pre-condition. As Mr. Crenshaw's attorney what would you advise?"

She knew he was right, but it was galling. "May I speak to my client first?"

"Yes."

"Alone."

Turning into a marathon but Jake acquiesced and left them. He was met by Buddy as he entered the break room to grab a cup of coffee and light up a cigarette.

"Having fun?" Buddy asked, big smile on his large face.

"You're watching that?"

"More fun than television. You realize she's pushing your buttons and do you know why?"

"I'm afraid no matter what I say I'm still going to be hit with your blinding insight."

"Because you push her buttons first, asshole. I don't know why she loves you or why anyone would."

"You're really reaching now. Where's the evidence she loves me?"

"You may be the dumbest white boy of all time and that's a lot because all you pale-faces are dumb about women. She's a strong, proud young lady and she's not going to allow you to vanish for months and then just pick things up where they left off. You stayed gone too long, Jake. You got a problem with expressing your emotions and you're doing that number again, where you avoid facing the topic, just like you did with your old man. Jake,

Harper loves you and you love her, but you're both too intractable to take the first step to resolve this thing. And as you are a rather pathetic and comical individual, and looking at Harper Bannister, a stone hottie with charisma, you should beg, no, you should run and beg for her to take you back."

Jake looked at Buddy for a long moment, and then said, "Do you feel better now?" Buddy nodded and then Jake said, "Okay, you're probably right."

"So, talk to her, stupid."

"Sure, do you want to hear about my visit to Senator Stedman?"

"Yeah, go ahead. What did he say?"

"Same as everyone else. He doesn't know anything, and his Lawyer is Charles Langley."

Buddy pursed his lips, thinking about that. "My god, they're closing ranks and trying to push us out."

"Exactly, and they've got the power to keep us at bay unless we can bust one of the weak links. There has to be someone involved that we can squeeze."

"Problem there," Buddy said, "is that the weak links may really not know anything. You have anyone in mind?"

"Well, first Rufus said it was Jimmy Davenport that gave him the money, but the source of the money was Colin Dukes, but that doesn't tell us much; hopefully Rufus has more to tell us; as for Davenport I can turn up the heat on him."

Buddy nodded in the direction of the interview room and then said, "You do that, and it'll cause trouble for you with Harper."

"Yeah, and right when I'm doing so well with her."

Buddy said, "I hear you."

CHAPTER 22

Rufus Crenshaw, with Harper present, revealed why he thought someone was following him. He even thought the man was following him to kill him or it was someone from the CIA after him because he knew some dirt on the agency. Rufus saying such things was exactly why he would make a poor witness during a murder trial.

"I didn't hit that car because I was drunk, my car wouldn't stop. I think my brake lines were cut."

Jake cut his eyes to Harper and then back to Rufus. "That sounds like something you saw in a movie, but we'll check it out. Is that all you have?"

"I seen a guy following me a couple times."

"Who?"

"I don't recognize him."

"Was it someone from the party?"

"Maybe, I don't know. He was driving an older car, like a Chevy."

"What kind of Chevy? What color? How old?"

"It was kinda off-white and had mismatched wheels. Looked like one of those Malibu cars about a 2004 or so. He drove by my place, too."

"Did you get a look at the driver?"

"Not a good one."

"Was it the man who gave you the money?"

Harper quickly jumped in and said, "Don't answer

that, Rufus."

"I'm trying to find a line to the killer of Cynthia Cross, I just want to know if the money is a pay-off leading to the killer. In a homicide, there are things that people have witnessed or done that shine some light on a string of evidence. I don't believe your client is involved but I want to know who gave him the money."

"It was Jimmy Davenport," Rufus said.

"Don't say anything else, Rufus," Harper said.

"That's something," Jake said, "You worried about your client or someone else?"

"We'll talk about that sometime, not now," she said.

"First, Rufus tells me why Jimmy gave him the money," Jake said.

"Does Rufus get immunity for this testimony?"

Jake nodded. "Yes, yes he does."

She struggled with it for a long moment before she said, "All right."

Jimmy Davenport gave him the money and told Rufus that he, Jimmy, would lock up the Country Club. So far, Jimmy Davenport hadn't lied, as he had said he locked up the place, but why the big pay-off to a small-time crook like Rufus Crenshaw?

"Did he say why he was paying you so much?" Jake said.

"I told him I was responsible, and he said it was okay, so he gave me the money and told me to go home. It's a lot of money, you know; how could I turn it down?"

"I understand that, but did he say why it was important that he lock up?"

Rufus looked at Harper who said, "It's okay."

Rufus wetted his lips, looked from Jake to Harper and back again, before he said, "Jimmy told me there were going to be things I shouldn't see and if I did, I might not be safe for me if I did."

Jake looked at Harper who was gazing off to the right and chewing the corner of her mouth, Jake said, "Sounds like I need to talk to your boyfriend."

"He's going to be out of town, today," she said. "Don't

give me that look, I don't know where he's going, he just said he had a meeting." She was quiet a moment and then she said, "Jake Morgan, if you open your mouth and say 'I told you so', there will be another homicide."

CHAPTER 23

They assembled at the home of Judge Preston Carmichael. In attendance were Senator Wyck Stedman, Frank Jankowski, Jimmy Davenport, Colin Dukes, and Mickey Wheeler. There was a dark mood.

"I did not enjoy my visit from this small-town deputy sheriff," Senator Stedman said.

Judge Carmichael opened up a second bottle of Blanton's Bourbon and everyone accepted a glass. Stedman and Carmichael had been drinking before the others arrived. Carmichael was uncharacteristically tipsy, and Stedman was nervous and angry.

The room was a large, open room in a modified A-Frame structure with a window wall that looked out on a small, man-made lake surrounded by seven figure homes smaller than Buckingham palace. The atmosphere in Carmichael's drawing room was tense, heightened by the low clouds threatening rain.

"He's more than a small-town deputy," Carmichael said. "My information is that he was an up-and-coming investigator with the Texas Rangers. Last year, he successfully stopped an armed bank robbery in Paradise, by killing one of them. Then, you may remember my friend, Vernon Mitchell, was investigated and his family's holdings decimated by this small-town deputy and Morgan accomplished both things without jurisdiction. Now Morgan has a badge and the backing of both the County and the City of Paradise so we gain little by underestimating the young man."

"He's got a mouth on him," Jankowski said. "He came around acting snotty, being a smartass, and insulted my family. You know my wife is the cousin of that woman he had an affair with and then he put her in prison."

"I would think it hard to insult you or your family, Frank," Stedman said, smiling hazily and taking another slash of the Blanton's.

Jankowski's lip curled and he said, "Watch yourself, Senator. You're not immune from shit."

"You going to assault me, Frank?" Stedman chuckled and some of his bourbon spilled. "Have you been watching the Godfather again? Settle down and try to access the non-thug part of your brain. Fucking football players. Shit."

Frank started to reply but Carmichael held up a hand and shook his head at the land developer.

Colin Dukes spoke up and said, "I don't care who this deputy is, we just need to keep our names out of the paper. I'm willing to fund an offer to him."

"That won't work," Davenport said. "You can't buy him. He's all hung up on some kind of hero complex. Goes way back. I've known him all my life and he's not going to stop prying," Davenport said. Davenport was uneasy as he had not always been privy to the working of the group, plus he was the youngest with the least power. Davenport noted that Dr. Thurgood had not been invited or refused the invitation. Neither was comforting. Davenport had been thinking about Morgan's return to town since the day in the Homestead restaurant, wondering if he had pushed his luck bragging about Harper. From what he remembered about Morgan, the guy was usually affable, which was an act, and never had been the type to overlook insults and would sneak up on you in conversation. "If you see him as a smartass or a small-town cop, he'll be laughing at all of us when he blows things up. He delights in that shit."

Mickey Wheeler, lounging on a bar chair, a cigarette dangling from the corner of his mouth, said, "You girls kill me. You're already nervous before you even know if he's after one of you. Glad I'm not one of you because I wouldn't like it if my nose bled every 28 days. But Jimmy D is right, this Morgan character, he ain't no pork chop. He's smarter than you guys, anyway."

"But, not you, right?" Dukes said.

Wheeler gestured at Dukes with his bourbon glass at Dukes, smiled and took a drag on his cigarette.

"Who said you could smoke in here?" Stedman said.

Wheeler took another languorous drag on his smoke and said, "I didn't ask. You kids better let Langley handle things and avoid interviews. You may be king-hell movers and shakers but this Morgan guy, I looked into him some. His last day with the Rangers he took out two cartel soldiers in a gun battle. Add that to the bank thing and well..." He paused to take a sip of bourbon. "What can I say to that?"

Stedman glared at Wheeler for a long moment, Wheeler smiled back, and said, "Senator, for all your education and your important friends, Morgan's will cut through your bullshit before you know it's happened."

"Why should we listen to you?"

Wheeler narrowed his eyes and lowered his head a quarter inch and said, "We all know why, and you'd best remember it."

Judge Carmichael said, "This isn't helpful. The problem at hand, as Mr. Wheeler pointed out, is that our careers are on the line and we are running scared, which is also accurate. There is a young woman —"

Wheeler interrupted the judge to say, "Named Kandy Kane."

Carmichael took a breath before continuing and said, "Yes, Miss Kane was killed, and we don't know who killed her, perhaps someone in this room but hopefully that is not the case, however the scandal could mushroom and become problematic for all of us." He stood and placed a finger alongside his cheek. "No, this must be handled carefully and with the right amount of finesse. Perhaps this Morgan will light on a suitable suspect and convict him without requiring any further intrusion into our lives."

"What're you saying?" asked Jankowski.

"There is the therapist, who I believe, was working with Miss Cross."

"I don't know the guy, but I know of him, and he looks soft like a guy who will fold under pressure, maybe the creep who did the girl," Jankowski said. "Wasn't me."

"No, just beat 'em up, don'tcha?" Dukes said.

"At least I don't let 'em piss on me. Heard that's the way you liked it, frat boy."

Davenport reached up and rubbed his shoulder. "Damn, let's not fall apart here. Nobody killed her in this room, right? I mean, surely not." At least, he hoped not.

"The body has been removed," Judge Carmichael said. "I commandeered the body under the auspices of a civil rights case she is now a part of."

"You don't think that raised a red flag for Morgan and Sheriff Johnson? Maybe you were a little quick to do something like that." Stedman then took a big slash on the bourbon and sloshed more into his glass from the bottle.

"Go easy on that," Carmichael said.

"Sure, dad," Stedman said, saluting the judge with the glass and then throwing back a good amount of liquor. "What about you, Jankowski?"

"I don't screw whores, Stedman."

Wheeler smiled and happily sipped bourbon at Jankowski's statement. Jankowski caught the smile.

"What are you looking at, Wheeler?"

Wheeler held up his glass and said, "Excellent bourbon."

Stedman saying now, "The question is do you have DNA on file, Frank? Real estate developers like you have a reputation you know."

"Fuck you," Jankowski said. "I don't have a criminal record and have never had to give up DNA."

"Enough of the bickering," Carmichael said. "We have an issue at hand, and we should be in concert about our response as it appears this Morgan and Sheriff Johnson are going to continue to pursue it."

"We're not responsible for her death, right?" Davenport said, not willing to use the M word. "We were all there at the Country Club and any contact we had and some of you in here did, they will continue to go at us."

"You had contact with her also, Davenport," Jankowski said.

"You said it was part of my..." Davenport's lips felt dry, he had his own suspicions, but they had drawn him into their circle, and he was trapped. "I didn't really like it."

"You didn't like it?" Wheeler said, smiling again.

Davenport ignored him and said, "If somebody here killed her then we've all got trouble." He stood and said, "I want no part of this anymore."

"Sit down, Jimmy," Jankowski said. "Quit being a pussy."

Colin Dukes had been sitting quietly, sipping bourbon but had become increasingly upset. "Goddammit! How did this get so out of hand, I mean, this isn't the first time we've had a party and now someone has lost their fucking mind and killed the girl. And I'm not sure it really wasn't one of the group." He looked directly at Mickey Wheeler.

"I had no reason," Wheeler said. "Had I a reason maybe, but she was a source of income for me and I'm a businessman."

"Yes, we've all heard about how you supposedly executed two men," Dukes said.

Wheeler touched his forehead with a finger and then saluted Dukes. "Something to remember."

"Gentlemen, no one had anything to do with her passing," Carmichael said. "She was a dancer and probably knew some unsavory characters."

"She was pretty choice for a 'dancer'," Wheeler said. "I think we can all agree on that."

Carmichael said, "It is an unhappy coincidence this death occurred and implicated us, and we were all there and therefore are 'persons of interest'. We must stay firm in our friendships and not allow the incident nor this Morgan to divide us."

"That's the first smart thing I've heard out of this bunch," Wheeler said.

"You mean we're going to stonewall this thing," Stedman said.

"That's one way," Wheeler said. "You could cooperate with Morgan and Sheriff Johnson, but looking around the room, you don't look like any of you could stand up to questioning, and admitting your mistakes is not something you guys are really into."

"I don't think that will be necessary," Carmichael said. "Just allow Langley to deal with this. He is an excellent attorney and has handled worse things."

"When?" Dukes said. "What is worse than this?"

"There are better ways," Jankowski said.

"Meaning?" Stedman said.

"I can't wait to hear this," Wheeler said, leaning back on the bar with his elbows on the bar. "Absolutely can't wait to hear what you 'respectable citizens' come up with. Hell, this is better than TV."

Harper didn't know where Jimmy Davenport's meeting was, but Rufus had a suggestion. "Judge Carmichael's lake house. They had me clean up the place one time after a party."

"Seems like you have quite a history with the judge," Jake said.

Jake borrowed a vehicle confiscated in a drug bust, a late model SUV, drove south and pulled into Lakeview Estates, a development of palatial homes on three acre lots, which Jake knew had been developed by Frank Jankowski.

Davenport's car was parked in the long drive leading to the home of Oliver Carmichael, father of Judge Preston Carmichael, along with several vehicles. Jake pulled over and parked in a spot that would afford him a good view of the house and settled in to wait.

"Looks like a party," Jake said, out loud. "Let's see who comes and who goes."

CHAPTER 24

Ninety-seven miles away from Jake's observation post, Deputy Gretchen Bailey walked back to her car after visiting the registrar's office of Missouri University. Bailey was at the end of a busy day of interviewing former students of Judge Oliver Carmichael and a few law students who may have heard of "Seek-and-Make".

"Seek-and-Make? Oh yeah," said a young man with longish hair and sunglasses. "Yeah, they're freaks, you know, but rich freaks with the juice to get away with it. Nasty bunch of dudes."

Another, a twenty-something coed wearing yoga pants and an Under Armour pullover told Bailey, "I had a friend dated one of those guys. At first, she was impressed but as the relationship grew, she realized he was really just a spoiled rich kid, and she said, 'he liked it rough'. She finally gave up trying to get rid of him and transferred to Missouri State."

She did not remember the man's name.

"You don't talk about those guys," said another student. "They're connected."

Bailey asked, "What do you mean by 'connected'?"

"I mean they have contacts out in the world with people who run things in the state and some who are big shots at a federal level."

"Give me a name."

The young man put his hands up and laughed. "Oh no, I know better than to get involved with this. My name comes back, and I'm done as a law student, and I can forget a career."

"They're that powerful?"

"Maybe they are and maybe they aren't, but a couple years back someone bucked them, a girl made a complaint to the administration about sexual harassment and attempted rape and...well."

"Well, what?"

"I don't know what happened to the girl, but I never saw her again. People said she was paid off and transferred schools."

"Do you remember her name?"

"Yeah, I think so. It was Melanie something. Wait, Melanie Braddock, that's it."

Bailey thanked the man and called Paradise County for a computer check on Melanie Braddock.

***

Sometimes Harper wanted to get out of the office.

"So, how're things going with you and Jimmy Davenport?" Sherry Hammersmith asked Harper. They were sitting inside the new Panera Bread Cafe out on the interstate where most of the new businesses were located. Harper, who did not want to talk about Jimmy which, with Sherry, and her own mindset, would eventually gravitate to Jake. Sherry was sweet but enjoyed putting her friend on the spot.

Harper had an argument last evening with Jimmy concerning Jake.

"Are you still seeing him?" Jimmy said, 'Him' meaning Jake.

"If I am, that would be my business, wouldn't it?" she told him.

"What about our relationship? Where are we going?"

"Why don't you tell me," Harper said, not telling him what Rufus Crenshaw had revealed, and then it had gone downhill from that point, Jimmy more agitated and worked up then normal. Plus, he showed up half in the bag, smelling of alcohol, reeking of it actually. Jimmy was a high energy person but lately seemed on edge and impatient.

"Well, come on, I need details, girl," Sherry said. "Do you have a future with Jimmy, or are you still mooning over the Jakester?"

"Sherry, you're a mess."

"Come on," Sherry said, mock pleading.

"Okay, Jimmy wants me to define our relationship," Harper said, in response to Sherry's question.

"And?"

"So, I did."

Sherry rolled her eyes and said, "You gripe about Jake's habit of being closed mouth and now you're doing it."

Harper laughed. "I'm doing that?" Shaking her head now and smiling. "And stop bringing up Jake's name. I know where you're going with that. Okay, I told Jimmy that we needed to date others and remain friends."

"Friends? Wow, the kiss of death." Sherry leaned back and made a face. "I'll bet he loved that."

Harper took a tiny sip of her salted Caramel cold-brew and said. "Incredibly, he did not 'love it'. He asked if being 'friends' meant a sexual relationship."

"And your response was?"

"Take a wild guess, Sherry. The ick factor on something like that is off the charts plus he thinks he can dictate where I go. Why are you so interested in this?"

"I don't have anything going right now. If romance was a liquid, my life wouldn't fit an ant's eye dropper. I want a little lust in the dust, some drama to liven things up in this town. Harper Bannister, you will never be the heroine in a romance novel. If you slept around maybe I could live life vicariously through your sexual escapades, during my drought, but you're a 21st Century yawn-fest."

"You're being ambiguous, as I know you've had every eligible male after you since middle school. I already divorced one jackass, I don't need another one."

"And then there's Jake Morgan," Sherry said, fluttering her eyelashes.

"Who is also a jackass of sorts."

"Yet not a total jackass and he is so cute and never chased after me, darn it."

"You seem to be the only one immune from that and he left town before we started menstruating. Sherry, does this conversation have anything like a point?"

"Let's see, we went to school together, we're best friends and I know you better than anyone, and you're drifting right now and the reason for this is that you have is a bad case of Jake Morgan."

"Well," Harper said. She shrugged and set down her cup. "I've always had that."

***

Jake sat in the borrowed SUV outside Oliver Carmichael's home when his cell phone buzzed. Gretchen Bailey. "This is Morgan, what's up, Bailey?"

"I checked on the people in question and also interviewed some students and faculty at MU law. I learned that 'Seek-and-Make' is a powerful secret fraternity within the fraternity system and they make people afraid. And here's something that will send a chill down your spine."

"What's that?"

"A young girl named Melanie Braddock made a complaint to the university against the 'Seek-and-Make' group. Soon after she disappeared from campus and six months later her body was fished out of the Gasconade River."

CHAPTER 25

Deputy Bailey's work gave Jake's homicide investigation another shot in the arm.

"You get anything on Cross' family?"

"No father but got a possible mother's name. Last name, Crane, first name, Sylvia. Haven't made contact yet but have last known address and will check back from there."

Jake thought about the ironic selection of her Mother's name as her alias. Who was Cynthia Cross trolling by using that name?

"That's good work, Bailey," Jake said. "See if you can get your hands on the autopsy report on the coed, who handled it and what jurisdiction? I owe you a beer at Hank's."

"How about a martini at the Homestead?"

"Okay, a martini. At Hank's."

"Hank's idea of a martini is a shot and a beer."

"Even better."

Jake heard her laugh. "You really know how to show a girl a good time."

"At least you didn't call me a male chauvinist."

"You've got that 19th Century macho thing going but you're no chauvinist. You treat everyone equally badly."

"Darcy amended the document on the Cross apartment, so I want you to head over that way and go through things, you know, look for address books, phone records, calendars and impound any computer you find. Call Medfield PD and see if they'll send a crime lab guy over to dust for prints, etc. I also need some photos of all the men who were at the party at the club to show to a possible witness, do you think you can scare some up for me?"

"I already have them. They're on your desk in a folder."

"What about the guy you had a line on? You know, one of the lesser ones, Adam Driver?"

"That was a dead end," Bailey said. "Literally a dead end."

"Murdered?"

"Medfield PD is calling it a break-in robbery gone wrong. He was found shot in his bedroom last night."

"Let's hope they're not thinning out our witnesses. We don't have much to go on as things stand."

"I haven't told you the best part yet," Bailey said. "I followed up on Philpott's death. I talked to Darcy Hillman who called the Pinnacle County PA and there was a document Pinnacle County had in their possession from Philpott that revealed the name of a man who paid for Cynthia Cross' apartment."

***

Jake settled in to surveil Judge Carmichael's house. Television stakeouts are two guys sitting in their car with a coffee thermos and exchanging funny lines or talking about their theory of life and baseball. In reality, every cop knew you didn't drink coffee because nature would call. Stakeouts were lonely and the boredom was soul-killing. Jake would play music on the radio, careful not to run the battery down, and try not to fall asleep. He wasn't there long before a neighbor tapped on his window and said, "Excuse me, sir, but this is a gated community. What are you doing here?"

Jake slapped the Paradise badge against the window and said, "Go back home."

The man left. The badge was good for some things.

An hour later, Jake watched Frank Jankowski and Senator Wyck Stedman drive away from the Carmichael estate. Jake waved at Jankowski as he drove by and Jake saw the red taillights flare up, then the brightness of back-up lights before Jankowski changed his mind and left.

Within minutes, a Missouri State Highway Patrol unit, an ice cream white Ford Explorer, pulled up. A trooper emerged from the vehicle, and the officer settled his Smokey the Bear hat on his head. His uniform was spotless and the crease in his slacks would cut paper, he was wide shouldered with weightlifter biceps pulsating under his blue shirt. Jake rolled down his window and said, "Hello, Ridley."

"Aw, hell, Morgan," Trooper Fred Ridley said. "I knew it would be you, hoped it wasn't, but I knew the only guy with the nads and the lack of discretion to sit outside Judge Carmichael's house would be you."

"Shh," Jake said, putting a finger to his lips. "You're blowing my cover."

"You're not hiding, so what are you doing? Is this about the Cross homicide?"

"Can't fool you, you trooper boys know everything, must be the training."

"Jake, as a personal favor, would you please get the hell out of here? You don't leave I'll just get another call and have to come back. You're cutting into my fun time terrorizing speeders."

"Who called you?"

"Someone called the lieutenant governor, who called my captain, who sent me out here."

"Well, well, well," Jake said. "I'm moving up in the world. All right, my work's done here anyway."

"So what did you think you'd accomplish?"

"See who was here and piss off the judge."

Ridley thumbed back the brim of his Smokey the Bear hat and said, "Well, you did that. You smell something, don't you, but be advised, the Carmichaels are clean-up hitters, both of them, and will slap you down. I hope you know what you're doing."

"What have I ever done that makes you think I know what I'm doing?"

"Go back to Texas, huh? My workload increases when you're around."

"I'll head out in a minute, but I need a favor."

Ridley raised his eyebrows and sighed. "I'm here to run you off and yet you believe you can make requests which I'll bet has something to do with why you're sitting here at the edge of the cliff and wanting me to give you a push."

"The name Melanie Braddock mean anything to you?"

Ridley nodded and said, "Yeah, it does. They fished her out of the Gasconade a couple years ago. Her family lives in Kansas City so I was picked to inform the family."

"I think she's connected, maybe only peripherally, to the Cynthia Cross homicide. I would appreciate it if you could get me her case file."

"It was ruled a suicide," he watched Jake momentarily, before saying, "but you don't believe that so I'll see what I can do. Is there anything else I can do for you? Never doubt I don't love being your go-fer."

"No, that's all I need." Jake flipped the back of his hand at his friend. "You may go now."

"Kiss my ass, Morgan, and get the hell out of here. You can't imagine the sense of joy I would feel snapping cuffs on you and duck-walking you to your own lock-up. I'd sell tickets and retire."

***

The last to leave the judge's home wasDavenport, and Jake tailed him to see where he went next.

Davenport drove back to Paradise and pulled into the parking lot of the Holiday Inn, which Davenport owned, got out and walked inside. Jake shut off his car and followed him inside to the hotel lounge, which was sparsely attended, just a pair of salesmen chatting up the waitress.

Davenport's server arrived with his drink just as Jake entered the lounge. Davenport started to take a sip, saw Jake approaching, closed his eyes, shook his head, and then took a long pull on his drink.

"Fuck," Davenport said. "It's you."

"Hello, Jimmy. Mind if I join you?"

"Will it make any difference?"

"No, but it'd make me feel better."

Davenport nodded at the seat.

Jake sat and said, "So, Jimmy, what're you doing hanging out at Judge Carmichael's with those other? Let's see, how did you describe them? 'outstanding citizens'? What're you whacky kids up to, planning a panty raid at the nursing home?"

"It was just a friendly visit, you know, a couple of drinks, a few laughs."

"And then because it was such a light-hearted time you immediately drove to a bar and decided to have a drink to drown your laughter. So, here you are, all alone."

"Maybe I'm meeting someone. Maybe someone you know."

"Could be," Jake said. "Maybe I'll hang around and see who that might be."

Jimmy sighed, threw back the rest of his drink, signaled the server, and pointed at his glass. "All right, I'm not meeting anyone, and you'll be happy to learn that Harper told me she just wanted to be friends."

"'Friends', ouch," Jake said, "The black curse of any relationship."

"Well, at least now you're happy."

"Have to admit, I'm not devastated, but I'm more concerned about your meeting with those fine people who may have raped and killed a young woman and then dumped her on a lonely dirt road. I am offended by that, and your buddies better understand that I am going to learn who did it and put them inside forever. You know, Jimmy, you're not the best little boy in the world, but I don't see you as a killer, but I think you have an idea who did. I know you well enough that I don't think you would kill anyone, but I've been wrong before."

The server brought Davenport another drink and asked Jake if he would like something and Jake requested a Dr. Pepper. The server left.

"Jake, you gotta believe me, I didn't have anything to

do with what happened to that girl."

"I do believe you," Jake said, wanting to get Davenport to open up. It really didn't matter what Jake believed, though he truly didn't think Davenport killed her, it only mattered that Jake accumulated information and evidence to learn who did kill her and whether anyone else was complicit in the crime of covering up. "But you'll have to start convincing me that you don't know more than you've told me."

"I can't."

"You were the last to leave Carmichael's house."

"The judge wanted to talk to me, and said it was important."

"How important?"

Davenport snorted, "Preston Carmichael says stay, you stay."

"What does the judge have to do with Cynthia Cross?"

Davenport dropped his eyes and swallowed as if something was stuck in his throat. He shook his head and then said, "Dammit, Jake, you don't know what you're getting into, or what you're asking me. I fucking can't do it."

"What about Jankowski? Your Ex, Rhonda, doesn't like the guy, says he hit on her."

"He's a loudmouth bully."

"You should have defended her honor."

Davenport snorted and shook his head. "Yeah? That's what she thought. The guy's big as a house and violent."

"Violent? How so?"

"Shit, you got me saying things. You're a sneaky guy, Jake."

"Accessory after the fact in a homicide carries a lot of weight and one way or another, I will find the person or persons who killed Miss Cross, and now is the time to talk to me, and when I do, I'm not sure you'll be able to stay clear. You need to talk now while you can make a deal. They're wearing drab grey prison outfits in Jeff City these days so I'd guess a snappy dresser like you won't care for that."

"Jake, this is dangerous shit. I say anything to you,

or someone knows I'm talking to you, and I could join Cynthia. You might think about that, yourself."

Jake finally getting somewhere.

"Jimmy, we can protect you. We'll hide you away and –"

"Ha! You think you can do that? Tell me, Jake, where is Cynthia Cross' body? Fuckin' tell me."

"How did you know about that?"

Davenport ran both hands through his hair. "Aw shit Jake, you're gonna get me killed."

"Talk to me, for your own good, and we'll see about getting you some immunity and protection."

Davenport chewed a thumb nail, looked around the room and said, "I've already said too much." He finished off his second drink and stood. "But I'll think about it, Jake. I really will."

With that, Jimmy Davenport stood shakily and staggered out of the bar, while Jake gave some thought to a DUI arrest, whereby he could shake Davenport some more and decided against that as it would not advance his relationship with Harper.

It troubled Jake that it was his first thought.

CHAPTER 26

Jake drove directly to Harper's house, hoping to catch her there, though he knew that might not be the best next move and it proved to be a mixed bag. She answered his ring but stood in the doorway like a palace guard.

"May I come inside?" Jake asked.

"Why?"

"I need to apologize for things I've done, or haven't done, and want to get it straight between us."

"Between us?" Harper said, cocking her head. "Wait, I'm going to have to get clarification. What does 'between us' mean?"

"Are you going to let me in or not?"

"I haven't decided." She paused for a moment, then moved aside and said, "Would you care for some coffee?"

Inside, Jake sat while Harper made coffee, and Harper's dog, a male Schnauzer named Bandit, jumped up in his lap. Jake stroked the dog's ears and said, "At least someone in this place likes me."

"Bandit is very egalitarian," Harper said, as she entered the room. Steam clouds wafted over the top of the coffee cups. "He pretty much likes everyone."

Harper handed Jake his cup and then sat across the room from him. "So, let's talk."

"I'm not sure how to start."

"You mentioned an apology."

"I thought I did that."

Harper shook her head and said, "I think you're a wonderful person, Jake. You're witty, but you're not accomplished at small talk and normal conversation because you don't have a normal life."

He shrugged and said, "I think small talk kills conversation and besides, we're talking now, aren't we?"

"If you can call it that. So, what brings you here tonight?"

"I just had a talk with Jimmy Davenport."

"And?"

"He's not down with the "friends" thing."

"So, you thought you'd come by and romance me with short declarative sentences that once again allow you to avoid saying anything of consequence."

"Is it working?"

"Not so far."

"How about I flex a bicep?"

She gave him a hard look. Jake sipped his coffee and met her gaze, watching her closely. She said, "Why do you believe you always have to have the last word?"

It was quiet for a moment before Jake said, "I didn't say anything."

"You don't say anything a lot even when you're talking. It's how you do 'the last word' and it's annoying."

Jake sipped his coffee and they looked at each other for a long moment.

Finally, Harper broke the silence. "What are you doing now, Jake?"

"Trying to avoid having the last word."

Harper stared at him for a moment and then fought the smile tugging at her mouth.

Jake continued, saying, "Also, watching for signs of attraction; see if your breathing picks up or your eyes dilate."

Harper shook her head, she had to admit he was funny. "Like I said, I think you're a wonderful man, Jake, that is, as far as being a macho shithead can take you. But if we were together again it would spoil everything for you because then you couldn't follow me around and see if I'm having fun."

"I'm not following you around."

"Really, then why talk to Jimmy?"

"Does Jimmy talk about Carmichael? Or Colin Dukes? Jankowski?"

"He doesn't like Jankowski. The others, I don't know. He didn't want to talk about meeting with that group at Senator Stedman's fundraiser."

"He ever say anything about the young woman who was killed, you know, mention her murder?"

She shook her head. "No. Funny that he didn't. I brought it up once, but he just said he was aware of it."

"But he told you I talked to him about it, right?"

"Yes."

"How did he feel about that?"

"He was upset that it happened at the Country Club and that it happened the night of some party he was at?"

"Did he tell you who attended the party or mention the words, Seek-and-make?"

Bandit jumped down from Jake's lap and scooted across the room to Harper. Harper patted the seat beside her and the little dog hopped up, circled twice, then curled up to rest his head on his paws.

"Was Jimmy involved in this murder?"

"I don't think so."

"You know, besides not liking Frank Jankowski, I don't think Jimmy liked the people he was hanging around with all that much, rather he saw them as useful contacts." She reached over and scratched under Bandit's chin and gave Jake a look. "You don't want to say anything bad about Jimmy, do you?"

"There's no reason for it. Can you think of anything he might have said, you never can tell what might be significant?"

She thought about it. Jake liked her look, it spoke of intelligence, compassion and honesty. "Where are you going with this, Jake?"

"I can't say."

The smile left her face. "This is another of those cop dodges where you tell me you can't comment on an open investigation, that it?"

"Something like that."

"Which means you don't trust me, right?"

Jake looked straight into her blue eyes and softly said, "Harper, I trust you more than anyone I've ever known."

That stopped her, thinking about it before she said, "Thank you."

"So?" Jake said, raising his eyebrows, inviting a response.

She shook her head. "Not yet."

CHAPTER 27

Sheriff Buddy Johnson called Jake and said, "C'mon, I'll buy you a beer at Hank's. As your supervisor, I give you leave to take a 45 minute vacation."

It was 4:30 in the afternoon when Jake met Buddy at Hank's. Jake was pleased to learn that Hank had brought his entry up to fire code standards.

"Fixed the door. That's better, Hank," Jake said.

"For who?" Hank said. "What can I get you two?"

Jake said, "I'll start off with a glass of water."

"Water?" Hank said. "I'm running a bar here. I look like Gunga Din to you?"

"No, Gunga Din is not nearly as charming," Jake said.

"Bring us two beers," Buddy said. "And a cheeseburger, I'm hungry."

"Two beers and a cheeseburger," Hank said, walking off mumbling. "My business is saved, I'll be a millionaire in a week."

Jake smiled and said, "Best thing about this place is Hank. Okay, Buddy, why are you buying me a beer?"

"I need to tell you something and I don't want you to go off half-cocked and start one of your rampages where you terrorize the community."

"How about it with the hyperbole?"

Buddy rubbed his forehead with a thumb and then said, "Jake, there is pressure mounting to take you off this homicide."

"What kind of pressure and from who? You mean the Carmichaels and the senator."

"I think you're catching on. Locals get that kind of pressure from high-rollers like Stedman and the Carmichaels and those with political ambitions leverage the heat with hoping for the promises of a happy future."

"Tell them you agree and take me off the case. Make it easy on yourself."

"No way, Jake," Buddy said. "I don't like pressure like that, and I hate people who think it will make me go their way. You sell part of yourself, they come back for the rest, so no, you go after them. If we get lit up, we burn down together."

"No, listen let it be known you ordered me off. This relieves the pressure on you and puts them off guard which will allow me to move around more easily. I'll still be with PPD. Get the word out that you assigned someone else and put me on 'administrative leave'. I'm used to that anyway."

"And people are likewise used to you doing what you feel like doing. Should I put Bailey on it?"

"She's the best you got but no, I need her as she's doing good background work and she doesn't need additional pressure. Tell the media we have no suspects and say we're working a cold case homicide for a woman named Melanie Braddock."

"Who is Melanie Braddock?"

Jake updated Buddy on the information obtained by Deputy Bailey.

Buddy said, "Bailey was not properly utilized by Sheriff Kennedy; good to see you realize her worth."

The door to the bar rattled and they watched Leo the Lion stare at it momentarily before attempting to push it again. Finally, Leo pulled it open.

"What did you do to your door, Hank?" Leo said. "For ten years I've been pushing it open and today you changed it."

"Ask your friend," Hank said. "The fascist back in the

corner with the black guy."

"Hank, you're a gem," Leo said. "Your warmth fuels this place."

Leo walked over to the ancient jukebox Hank kept filled with equally dated music and then joined his friends at their table.

An Eagles tune about 'Too Many Hands' swelled from the juke. Leo sat and said, "How goes the war against crime?"

"Crime's winning," Jake said. "And Buddy may have to fire me."

"Why would you do that, Buddy? I mean, I know why I would do that but I'm interested in knowing why you would do that."

"You could help by getting the word out," Buddy said.

Leo looked at Jake, then back at Buddy. "What're you two guys up to now?"

"Fighting crime and dodging bullets," Buddy said.

"You got anything for us, Leo?" Jake said.

"I do. As your CI, I will expect remuneration for this information."

"While the fact the school actually pays you to do a poor job of coaching may be considered 'criminal' you do not fit the classic definition," Buddy said. "Be a good citizen."

"This is diamond hard, solid gold intel. James Bond's got nothing on me so we're talking two beers and a hot dog."

Buddy looked at Jake who shrugged, then said, "Pay the man."

Buddy shook his head and made a face, "I'm trying to remember the last time you picked up a tab, Leo."

"You're lucky the Lion hangs around with dolts. A certain local shrink contacted me and said he heard I was a friend of Jake's. For the sake of the information, I pretended to like you, Morgan, though it rankled."

Buddy put his head down on his palm and said, "Dammit, Leo, just say it."

Leo lifted his chin imperiously and said, "You have no appreciation for genius. That is a hallmark of the illiterate."

***

Jake was behind on his chores at the farm due to his dual authority with the city and the county. He hired a housekeeper to come in twice a week and a high school kid to feed and water the cattle. Most of the 225 acres of farmland he had rented out as he didn't have the time to plant himself. Jake was at the point where he wondered if he would have to sell the place where he grew up, but he still enjoyed the ambience of farm living and the isolation which allowed him to take in beautiful mornings and equally lovely evenings, sitting on his front porch and looking out across the land.

He still liked to sit on the deep front porch and listen to music, liked the smells of country living and the deep quiet of the farm, cattle lowing, that sort of thing.

Nothing going with Harper, getting nowhere in the murder investigation, and Jake knew he could easily lose his job no matter what Buddy said or did. His life was at a standstill.

Jake replaced the old storm door with a new one he'd purchased at Mannheim's Hardware and had cleaned out the gutters with a garden hose. He would have gotten a better price at Home Depot, but Jake liked shopping locally and the reason he bought his groceries at Sholl's Market, in what people called 'Oldville'.

Leo the Lion's talk with Dr. Drake Thurgood was helpful and Thurgood wanted an audience with Jake but not in public, so Jake called Thurgood at his office, Thurgood telling him that during his sessions with Cynthia Cross she had revealed that Frank Jankowski and Colin Dukes had both availed themselves of her services. Further that Dukes had become infatuated with her and wanted to be her exclusive client.

"This is a violation of my oath of privacy," Thurgood said. "Please do not reveal me as a source."

"Are you willing to testify?"

"Only as a last result," Thurgood said. "I am at risk if the wrong person learns I shared this."

"Who is the wrong person, Dr. Thurgood?" Jake said.

"That's all I have. For now. Please do not contact me again. But, if it is absolutely necessary, send word through Mr. Lyon. I must go now."

Leo was right. It was good information and spoke of motive for both Jankowski and especially Dukes. Dukes wanted an exclusive relationship. Was Dukes the mystery man Meryl Strip had mentioned?

It was twilight when he finished fitting the screen door, so Jake rolled up the hose, grabbed a beer out of his fridge, and sat on his porch. Clouds were building in the south and air was thick with ozone. He was deciding whether or not to fire up a cigarette, arguing against it, when his cell phone buzzed.

He was surprised to get a phone call from a panicked Jimmy Davenport. "Jake, I need to talk to you about some things."

"I'm listening."

"Not over the phone. Just come over to my place, and hurry. I've been thinking and this thing is a mess and you're going to want to hear what I have to say but I only tell you. I'm in a lot of fucking trouble and I want immunity."

"Look, Jimmy –." Davenport had hung up.

Jake changed clothes, dropped a hideaway Smith and Wesson Nine in his pants pocket and then took his pickup to town rather than the Mark IV. It began to rain; lightly at first, then pelting his windshield. Jake called Buddy to report where he was headed, couldn't raise him, so he left a message and then called dispatch and told the operator to contact Buddy and tell him, "I'm on my way to interview Jimmy Davenport at his home."

Jake's farm, left to him by his father, was ten minutes north of town. He gave some thought to calling Harper to see if she could shine any light on Davenport's state of mind but rejected it thinking that she might see it as an attempt to contact her under false pretense. On the radio there were severe thunderstorm warnings and the wind and rain lashed against the frantic beat of the windshield wipers.

The rain had settled into an anvil chorus by the time Jake arrived at Jimmy's tidy three-bedroom home in an older neighborhood. Jimmy's half-million dollar, gated, four-bedroom home on the other side of town was presently occupied by his ex-wife Rhonda where Jimmy was persona non grata.

Jake made another attempt to call Buddy before he got out of his pickup and got him this time, the sheriff telling him dispatch had contacted him.

"Did Davenport say what he wanted to tell you?" Buddy asked. "I'll head that way."

"No, he said he would only give the information to me. He was scared so I figured it has to do with our investigation."

"Sounds like a set-up."

"Way ahead of you but with Dr. Thurgood and now Jimmy their united front is cracking. Things are picking up."

Jake exited his pickup, walked up, and rang the doorbell. When there was no response, he knocked on the door. Still no response. Jake dialed up the number Davenport had called from, and it went straight to voice mail.

Jake pulled the Smith and Wesson, and walked around to the back of the property, but found nothing. Jake returned to the front door, tried the doorknob, which was unlocked, turned it and stepped inside.

"Paradise Police," Jake said, as he entered. "Jimmy, are you here? Jimmy Davenport."

Jake moved from the front room through to the kitchen, and then down the short hallway leading to the bathroom and two bedrooms. He found nothing in the first bedroom or the bathroom. When he stepped into the master bedroom he saw Jimmy Davenport sprawled on the floor, a man's belt around his neck. Jake kneeled to check Davenport's pulse and there was nothing.

Davenport was gone.

Jake called dispatch and was told that "Sheriff Johnson is on the way to that address". Jake told dispatch to get hold of Wiley the photographer and clicked off.

That done, Jake gave the room a good look, careful not to touch any surfaces and backed out of the room. He called Dr. Zeke and Zeke told him he'd be there "directly". Jake snapped some photos of the room and of Davenport and moved through the house, taking more photos but would still want the professional work Wiley could afford the investigation.

Jake returned to his pickup and lit a cigarette, waited for Buddy, Zeke and Wiley to show. Jake was sure the Cabal that made up 'Seek-and-Make' had decided to terminate Jimmy's membership.

And the killer had taken Jimmy Davenport's cell phone, which is why his call was terminated, which meant there would be text messages and phone calls to other members of Seek-and-Make they didn't want known. Worse, the killer likely had Harper's cell number.

Dr. Zeke did his examination, Wiley took his photos and Deputy Bailey marked off the crime scene with police tape. Jake spent the time going over the exterior of the home, lighting the grounds with his flashlight. The rain had stopped, and he hoped the damp ground would afford him a footprint or he would get lucky. It would be easier if killers would leave business cards, but he didn't expect that.

Jake told Buddy about Davenport's call and their talk at the Holiday Inn bar. "Jimmy was about to roll over on someone," Jake said. "Looks like they didn't trust him to keep quiet." Shaking his head now. "Well, at least we'll be able to get Jimmy's DNA."

"You think he killed the stripper?" Buddy said.

"No, but we'll know if he had sexual intercourse with her. That will eliminate one of them."

"You know, if we get a DNA match, the press is going to say Jimmy was the killer."

Jake nodded and said, "Yeah, I'm afraid you're right and it bothers me, even think that could be why they executed him. But he didn't do it, Jimmy's not the type for it."

"Everybody's the type for it," Buddy said.

"Jimmy was overpowered and strangled with his own belt. We'll have to wait for an autopsy to see if there is anything else."

"There are going to be some who will say you did it over Harper. Do you have the timestamp Jimmy phoned you on your cell?"

"Yes."

"That will take care of that, so, who do you like for this?" Buddy asked.

Jake had been thinking about that while he waited for the forensics team to show. "I don't know. The first one was a crime of hatred and passion, this one is a cover-up, so it doesn't necessarily have to be the same person, but it could be. Nearly everyone on our list has reason to want Cynthia Cross dead or at least shut up. Now, the killer either knew Jimmy was going to flip or they suspected it. They may have learned that Jimmy talked to me at the Holiday Inn or didn't like seeing him sitting with me and his ex, Rhonda at the Country Club."

"You were with his ex-wife at the Country Club?"

"Yeah, he was with Harper."

"What are you, swingers? Why does it seem to me that you live a weird life?"

"You should see it from my perspective, Buddy. Hell, it's worse than you can imagine."

CHAPTER 28

Senator Wyck Stedman called Oliver Carmichael, father of Judge Preston Carmichael and said, "Someone killed James Davenport, you may remember him from the fund-raiser last May."

"Yes, I do remember him, a young man on his way up, and that is a terrible thing. Why is this important to me?"

"We have a situation here you probably are not aware of that involves your son, Preston," Stedman said, and then shared the scenario at the Country Club, the murder of the young lady and the subsequent investigation.

When Stedman finished, Oliver Carmichael asked, "Did you kill her?"

"Of course not."

"Did my son kill her?"

"We don't know who killed her or why but the scandal, Oliver, is devastating."

"All right, I'll see what I can do."

Oliver Carmichael rang off and knew he had much to do. He unlocked a drawer on his home office desk and retrieved a different cell phone to make his calls. It may be time to cut his losses and protect himself and his son.

***

Jake had not forgotten about Colin Dukes, an interesting name on the list of people who attended the last dance of Kandy Kane. Dukes had been away on a business trip and the meeting at Judge Carmichael's home was the first time Jake knew Dukes was back. Jake wanted to move quickly before Dukes settled in, so he arrived at Dukes' office in Medfield early the next morning.

Colin Dukes was the CEO of Dukes Development, which built most of the parking lots and shopping centers in the area and employed hundreds of workers. Colin Dukes was the impetus and had designed the Pinnacle County Industrial Park which included a UPS distribution center, A Hobby Lobby warehouse, and a Folger's Coffee distributor in addition to several other businesses. The Dukes' building was the centerpiece of the complex; a gleaming cube of glass and steel fronted by a wide lawn featuring a geometric sculpture and fountain.

Jake walked through a glass door, into the hushed interior, and asked for "Mr. Dukes". Jake was escorted to a waiting area and the receptionist told Jake she would tell Mr. Dukes that he was here. But, before Jake sat, the door to the office opened and surprise, out walked Mickey Wheeler.

Wheeler stopped, gave Jake a sly James Dean look, smiled and said, "What a coincidence."

"That's what this is?" Jake said. "I think you beat me to him and I'm wondering why a struggling garage owner would be here visiting a high-speed go-fast entrepreneur like Colin Dukes?"

"I read in the paper that you had another homicide in your little town and I'm thinking, gee, what a hotbed of crime Paradise has become. Sad to see this in a cute place like Paradise. Poor old Jimmy D., hate to see it." Wheeler placed a hand over his heart. "May he rest in peace. Have you solved it yet?"

"Standing here looking at you, I feel I'm getting closer."

Wheeler wagged a finger at Jake and said, "Now, now, let's not get all harsh and ruin our relationship."

"You're jumping to conclusions, Mick. Perhaps I mean

Mr. Dukes, or you know, maybe a senator, or even a judge. Still, here you are, once again, right in the middle of things." Jake cocked his head and wagged a finger at Wheeler. "If I didn't know better, I might start thinking you have knowledge of this affair and are taking steps to cover everything."

"Sure would like to help you out, law and order, that's me, but I don't know anything."

"Maybe a subpoena will jog your memory," Jake said. "In fact, I have one warming up in the bullpen for you and all your circle jerk buddies. Tell me, how is it a guy like you, why are you hanging around with all the cool kids, Mickey? You just don't fit in."

Wheeler gave Jake a Cheshire Cat smile and said, "You know, back when I was in Jr. High, this big guy told me to give him my lunch money, but I didn't have any money on me. He said I would have to take a beating, so I kicked him square in the balls. Got suspended from school but he never asked me for my lunch money again. Now, did I just not have any lunch money, or did he decide to look elsewhere?"

Jake shook his head and said, "Great story. But I'm not after your lunch money, just your lifestyle."

"And you're right, like you said, you have your piece with you."

"And it's loaded."

"Sounds like a threat," Wheeler said.

"I don't make them. Never have."

Wheeler raised his chin, smiled and said, "Well, you have a nice day and good luck with your killings."

And with that, Mickey Wheeler turned, whispered something to the receptionist who laughed, and he left the building.

Colin Dukes was a square-jawed middle-aged man, tan with a barber-trimmed mustache; the kind of guy who probably had his way with the girls back in college, but middle age was creeping over his belt. His office was modern; glass and chrome, some tasty impressionist art on the wall along with an aerial photograph of a shopping center which Dukes Inc. had developed.

"Mr. Dukes, I'm Jake Morgan, Paradise County Sheriff's Investigator. I'm hoping you can help me out by answering a few questions."

"I don't think so," Dukes said. "Besides, you no longer have standing with Paradise County."

"My administrative leave doesn't begin until tomorrow. Funny you should know about that though. I guess I'm wondering who told you as that will help me unravel this thing."

"You'll have to refer them to my attorney, Charles Langley of –."

"Langley, Pope and Hardy," Jake said, finishing it for him. "You seem jumpy, when you don't even know what I'm inquiring about, maybe I have a business proposition for you, but I figure that's why Mickey Wheeler was here. Wheeler gets around, doesn't he? Still it surprises me that you and he are such close friends."

"We're not friends," Dukes said, too quickly.

"Not friends, then why was he here?"

"Business deal."

"What kind of business? Quite a bit of what Wheeler does to turn a buck is unethical, even immoral. Do you know a young woman named Cynthia Cross? You may know her as Kandy Kane or read about her in the paper concerning her homicide after a party you attended."

Dukes cold-stared Jake, something he probably reserved when dealing with employees. Jake picked a piece of lint off his sleeve while Dukes dialed his phone and said, "Denise, get me Charles Langley's office, please." He hung up the phone, folded his arms across his chest and looked at Jake.

Dukes' phone buzzed, he picked it up and said, "Dukes." Pause. "Yes, he's here now." There was a long pause. "Okay, I'll tell him." Dukes hung up the phone and then said to Jake, "My attorney says we'll wait for the subpoena. In fact, he said he doubts you can obtain one, but we will talk only with him present. Right now, I have work to do and appointments to keep so I'll have to ask you to leave, please."

So, not today with Dukes, but soon. They were getting antsy but Jake thinking, you can't strike out if you never get up to the plate.

***

The next morning was Saturday so Jake agreed to meet Leo the Lion for breakfast at the Dinner Bell. First, he wanted to check-in with Darcy Hillman to find out if there was any movement to interview the people on his list and he wanted to follow up with Dr. Zeke.

Darcy Hillman didn't have good news.

"Langley is dragging his feet," the PA said.

"This is a homicide investigation. Push him a little."

"He doesn't like you and doesn't want you to do the interviews."

"Fine, let Buddy do it."

"Buddy says no," Darcy said. "The sheriff says you're the guy with the experience they hired to do it and told Langley to fly a kite."

Good ol' Buddy.

Dr. Zeke had better news telling Jake they had a DNA match.

"Davenport was a match for a semen sample," Zeke said. "Looks like he had sex with the victim."

"Figured that would be the case. Still, I don't see Jimmy as a killer or a rapist."

"Yeah, well they're going to holler for you to close out this thing. People like expedient endings."

"Thanks for getting back to me on this," Jake said. "That was fast."

"Judge Carmichael got the lab to fast-track the information, and says we need closure for the public. Unusual for a man of his stature taking an interest, isn't it?"

"Could be just what he says it is, but I believe what it really means is there will be a big push to pin the Cross murder on Jimmy and pressure for me to close out the investigation. But no matter what they're hoping, this is not over. Someone killed Jimmy and it wasn't me."

These things were on Jake's mind when he met Leo for breakfast and Leo said, "You want my take on this?"

Jake watched a couple of farmers he knew walk into the restaurant. They waved to Jake and Leo. Jake sat and looked out the large plate glass window, with "The Dinner Bell" printed. On the inside the letters were reversed, the morning light slipped between the letters and printed on the floor. Jake stared at the reversed logo for a long moment before he said, "Yeah, go ahead, can't hurt. I feel like I'm missing something."

"Maybe you're overthinking it," Leo said. "You do that, always have. Sherlock Holmes says, if I remember correctly, 'you should concentrate on logic rather than upon the crime'. You have a lot of people involved in this thing but you're wondering which string to pull."

Jake considered his friend and nodded his head. "How do you remember an obscure Sherlock Holmes quote?"

"I read; you should try it. Maybe you need to drop back and punt. Go at this puzzle from another angle. You're looking for a rapist and a killer but maybe there is something else at work here. Clear your head and take a different tack, or knowing you as I do, you will also continue to bow-dick your life, worse than it is," Leo said to Jake, the two long-time friends seated at the Dinner Bell Cafe. "Pass me the half-and-half, please."

"It is my settled decision to resume my life as a gentleman farmer and become an alcoholic. I have some practice, besides what could be better than fake administrative leave with real pay, it's like a dream vacation?" Jake said. He stirred a second sugar packet into his grits then pointed at Leo's plate of biscuits and gravy. "Look at what you're eating? I can hear your arteries harden from here. No creamer for you, you're getting gooey around the middle. Drink your coffee black like a real man."

Leo leaned across the table and snatched up a creamer cup before Jake could move it away. "I am only five pounds over my high school playing weight and it's none of your business if I have cancer," Leo said. "Who're you to talk, Mr. Sugar Packets? Why would I heed health advice from a murder suspect? And you hate vacations. If there's shit to be stirred, you will always be on hand with the spoon. Do you have any idea who, I hate even saying the words, who killed Jimmy?"

The door opened and the sweet scent of early morning swept into the café. Voices of the new day scattered and chased each other. Forks scraped plates and chairs scooted across tile.

"Several," Jake said. He swirled the grits with a spoon. "But I don't have much on any of them and they won't talk to me. I'll probably spend the next couple days puttering around the farm, golfing, or hiding out from my fans in the media."

"I don't believe that any more than you believe that. You're not going to leave this thing alone, and as your mentor I advise you to not read this morning's paper, Jake, it'll just upset you."

"Give me the condensed version."

Leo spooned creamer into his coffee and stirred. "They're saying it's the second Paradise murder and you're an incompetent investigator involved in a love triangle with the victim."

"Wow."

"Oh, and you were the last person in contact with the victim and there is mounting pressure to have you removed."

"Removed from the investigation?"

"More like removed from the face of the earth."

"That sounds about right," Jake said.

"How're things with Harper?"

"About like my investigation."

"You are only summer to her heart and not the full seasons of the year."

"Is that Tennyson or Leo the Lion?"

"Edna St. Vincent Millay, Sugar Packets."

Jake stared at Leo for a long moment, spooned some grits and said, "Just eat your breakfast, fatty."

CHAPTER 29

Jake sat in Buddy's office as the evening turned late. Chief Bannister had come by to visit the two men. The clock on the wall showed eleven.

"Jake," Cal said. "The mayor and the city council met in a special session last night and wanted to suspend you with pay for two weeks, starting on Monday. I objected, pointing out that what they're doing isn't right and they didn't have a quorum because a couple of the members weren't in attendance. I told them if they proceeded, they would have my resignation, effective at the end of the month."

Jake sat up in his seat and said, "Don't do that, Cal."

"There are some on the council, pumped up by that idiot, Cecil Vanguard, to fire you. He wants a vote on it at the next city council meeting; that damned Cecil is on Senator Stedman's campaign committee. This is bullshit, Jake."

"You resign that clears the way for them to appoint a puppet and this thing will never be resolved and you know that's true. While I appreciate the gesture, you need to be proactive and suspend me, with pay of course so I can continue to pursue my lavish lifestyle and then hang tough until we can flush the killer out."

Buddy turned in his chair to address both men and said, "I'm being pressured to clear the Cross investigation. Davenport's DNA match makes him an easy target, but we all knew that was coming. The word around the Country Club crowd is that Davenport killed her, and the DNA proves it."

"It's too easy," Jake said. "And, once again, Judge Carmichael intervenes in the investigation, and he is the only person who could get the info out about the DNA."

"Carmichael can make people believe he's just a good citizen," Buddy said. "If I wasn't involved in this, I would never believe he was part of a cover-up. He's got a hell of a reputation in the community so, you're right, something stinks about this for him to take such an active interest."

"Davenport's DNA wasn't the only one Dr. Zeke picked up."

"We'll have a tough time selling a subpoena on the others to any judge. No one will want to buck Carmichael."

"We could ask them to volunteer; appeal to their sense of service to the community." Jake looked at both men, shook his head and said, "And then I'm going to buy a lottery ticket." He nodded at Cal and said, "First I will need you to rescind your resignation."

"Well," Cal said. "We got a few days until they meet again, so I guess you'll just have to hurry up and solve this thing."

"I'm on leave with both you and the county."

"Never stopped you in the past and I already talked to Buddy about your little scam pretending you're off the case. You two scamps are worse than junior high kids."

"The pressure from these people further convinces me Jimmy Davenport didn't kill her."

"But he did have intercourse with her," Buddy said.

"Yeah, but so did maybe three other men. And we still don't know if one of the rapists is the killer, but it would be a hell of a coincidence. No, something doesn't feel right."

Cal's intercom beeped and dispatch came on to announce, "There's a bunch of teenagers gathered at the park. There was a scuffle and underage drinking."

"I got it," Jake said, and left the office, glad to have something to do, something to change the subject.

The "bunch of teens" turned out to be five boys, all of them high school football players and the fight was just clowning around, but the beer was real. Jake drove his F-150 pickup, rather than the city unit, so he could get close knowing the boys might scatter if they saw the city car. When Jake exited the truck, the boys looked at each other and started to go 'rabbit'.

Jake held a hand up. "Hang on," Jake said. "If you run it'll piss me off, besides I'll just run the plates on your vehicles and get you later. Give me the beer."

"We don't have any beer," said a dark-haired kid Jake recognized as William Osborne.

"Willy, I know you have it, just give it up and I'll let you go."

"What're you gonna do to us?" Willy said.

"You're too old to spank and I'm too tired to drag you downtown, so hand it over and don't hesitate."

The young men handed him a six-pack holder with one missing. Jake held out a hand, flexed his fingers and said, "All of it, c'mon."

Jake scored two more six-packs and an unopened pint of Jim Beam. Jake poured the booze out on the ground and dumped the cans and the bottle in a park trash can. Jake said, "All right, fellas, hold up your right hand and repeat after me."

"Aw, c'mon Mr. Morgan, that's stupid."

"Okay, put your hands behind your backs while I get out the cuffs, and then I'll have Coach Lyon deal with you." Jake saw the hesitation in their faces. Kids, huh? "No?" All five held up their right hands and Jake said, "I promise to quit being stupid enough to drink beer in public again, so help me God."

They chanted it back to him and he added another line.

"And we promise to be good little dorks and wear clean underwear."

They didn't repeat that and instead groaned and shook

their heads. Well, you can't have everything but you gotta have fun sometime. He sent the boys home and returned to his pickup when he saw the off-white 2005 Chevy Malibu with mismatched wheels drive slowly by.

It was the car that Rufus Crenshaw had described to him.

CHAPTER 30

"Dispatch, this is Morgan, I'm in pursuit of a white Chevy Malibu with Illinois Dealer plate, DL 977A, northbound On Hwy 27."

Jake had followed the Chevy to see if the driver would roll past Rufus Crenshaw's place, instead the Chevy drove down the street where Harper Bannister lived and then slowed noticeably in front of her home. At that point, Jake placed his portable police light on top of the pickup and lit the candles. The Chevy did not stop, but rather took off at a high rate of speed.

"Will need assistance," Jake said to his radio mike. "Again, White Chevy Malibu, mismatched wheels north-bound on 27, passing Clearwater and gaining speed."

The Chevy sped forward at a greater speed than Jake had figured on, meaning that whatever the car had under the hood wasn't stock. Jake's F-150 pickup was made for hauling and driving across rutted fields and though it generated 365 horsepower when the turbos kicked in, he was no match for whatever the Malibu had under the hood.

The radio crackled and dispatch said, "The Dealer plate is a fake. Deputy Makepeace is in route for assistance."

Jake knew chasing a hopped-up car in his pickup was going to be futile if he didn't get help. Jake stomped the pedal, and the turbochargers pushed the big truck faster, but he couldn't close the gap. As they passed the Paradise

City Limits sign, a railroad crossing on a slightly raised grade, loomed like an Evel Knievel jump ramp.

The Malibu never slowed, and Jake saw the wheels of the vehicle leave the pavement and clear the tracks like an Olympic skier.

"Well," Jake said, out loud, to himself. "If he can do it..."

The pickup hit the raised tracks hard and the heavy truck bounded up and hit the ground on the other side of the tracks. The F-150 lurched sideways on impact and there was a sick moment when the front end leaned left, and the rig spun a half-circle before sliding into the ditch. Jake kept the wheels turning and tried to right the vehicle, but the rear end continued to plow dirt. Jake switched to four-wheel drive and with the front wheels engaged he was able to return the truck to the pavement.

The Chevy was long gone.

Jake returned the truck to two-wheel drive and drove out into the rural areas hoping to see dust plumes on side roads or perhaps the driver wrecked the Chevy, but no luck. Jake considered calling out to the Highway Patrol but he really didn't have anything to pin on the driver. What would he tell them, that he was chasing the Chevy for driving slowly by his girlfriend's home, when she presently wasn't his girlfriend? Further, Jake had no standing as he was on faux administrative leave and the Highway Patrol could not acknowledge transmission from him.

First thoughts. One, the fake license suggested criminal activity. Secondly, the Chevy Malibu was an older car that had been enhanced with a high-powered engine and a heavy-duty suspension which suggested someone who had the capability of souping up a vehicle which suggested Mickey Wheels' garage. Third, before Jake would be able to obtain a warrant, Wheeler's employees would have torn down the vehicle into parts, and investigating parts registration numbers was a time-consuming affair.

Rufus Crenshaw had twice given good intel about Davenport and now about the White Malibu, but that was perhaps the extent of what Rufus could provide. Jake knew he should have merely followed the Chevy but when the driver slowed in front of Harper's home, Jake made a rash decision and now, that link in the investigation would likely be gone.

Jake's investigation was going nowhere. He thought about Leo the Lion and the Sherlock Holmes quote. What had he missed?

Time to start over.

CHAPTER 31

Hillary Edson, AKA: 'Meryl Strip' lived at Bent Oaks, one of those singles' apartment complexes with a swimming pool and a small exercise room filled with a universal weight machine and a half-dozen treadmills, landscaped with trees and bushes. There was a laundry room and hot-and-cold running desperation.

Hillary lived on the second floor of one three-story building, apartment 211. Jake had brought along the packet of photos Deputy Bailey had prepared. He knocked on the door and there was no answer, so Jake knocked again and said, "It's Jake Morgan, remember me?"

"Go away."

"I just want to show you some pictures. No big deal, just look at them and I'll leave."

"I can't."

"Sure you can. Come on, open up."

He heard the metallic sound of safety locks being moved and she said, "Come on in while I put something on."

Jake entered the apartment. It was clean and well-ordered but dark inside. There was a large, framed photo of Marilyn Monroe on one wall and a big screen TV, faint odor of marijuana over the masking scent of a sugar-and-vanilla candle which burned and flickered on a coffee table strewn with fashion magazines.

Jake stood and waited for Hillary to return, and he was surprised by the change from Meryl Strip to Hillary Edson. No makeup and she wore designer jeans and a smart cotton blouse, made her look like the girl-next-door, but the look was marred by the plum-colored discoloration under her left eye and the swollen lip.

"Who did that?" Jake said.

She shrugged, chewed her lower lip on the side that wasn't puffy and said, "Goes with the job."

He didn't believe her; Jake was more of a mind that it was a consequence of talking to Jake at the Gentleman's Club.

"Was it Hoss?"

Hillary lowered her eyes and said, "What difference does it make? I like you but I can't talk to you. Please understand."

Jake produced the Manila folder and said, "So, don't talk. Point out which of these men looks like Cynthia's secret boyfriend who kept her in a two grand a month apartment."

She sighed and shook her head. "I told you I didn't get a good look at him, but okay, I'll try."

Jake asked if he could use the dining room table and she said, 'okay' so they moved to the small table and Jake fanned out the photos on the tabletop, one at a time. First, Jimmy Davenport, then Dr. Drake Thurgood, followed by Colin Dukes, then a couple of men Deputies Makepeace and Bailey had interviewed and no reaction. When he showed her the photo of Frank Jankowski, Hillary sucked in her breath and recoiled.

"Is it him?" Jake asked.

She shook her head quickly. "No."

"Why are you reacting this way if it's not him?"

She nodded and looked at the photos. "The boyfriend is shorter, much shorter."

"But you know Jankowski?"

She nodded.

"This is Frank Jankowski," Jake said and pointed at her eye. "I'm going to guess he's the guy who gave you that."

"Is that all of your pictures?"

"I have one more." He threw down the photo of Judge Preston Carmichael and she looked at it for a long moment, before picking it up and looking closer. "This one," she said. "He looks familiar, like someone else I've seen. I can't place him right away. No, wait. Oh, shit...this looks like Cynthia's daddy when he was a young guy."

***

Frank Jankowski had been into the Gentleman's club more than once. "He thinks he's a hobbyist," Hillary had told Jake. When Jake looked confused, she told him a 'hobbyist' considers himself a connoisseur of strip clubs and prostitutes.

"He's a beater," she added. "A sadist."

Jankowski gave Hillary the black eye but that was nothing new. The girls didn't like Jankowski, but Hoss told them the boss, meaning Mickey Wheeler, had given Jankowski 'privileges', and Jankowski tipped big. "A couple of the girls who don't mind turning tricks take care of him. I'm a dancer, not a whore and that's what I told him and why he gave me this." She pointed at her eye.

One more link between Jankowski and Wheeler besides the Country Club incident and the photo of Judge Carmichael made the gears spin in Jake's head. Wheeler was a lowlife, but he was smart and knew how to exploit the weaknesses of others. If Jankowski was a frequent shopper of strippers, then Wheeler had the developer in his pocket.

Was Wheeler blackmailing others in 'Seek-and-Make' or just Jankowski? It was logical speculation that Wheeler had something on more than one of them and maybe all of them.

"What if I could guarantee you'll never see Frank Jankowski again?"

"How would you do that?"

Jake now had a way to legally get Frank Jankowski's DNA and maybe force the man to testify against his buddies.

Sometimes the smallest things work out.

CHAPTER 32

1 A.M., in Medfield, a fingernail moon peeked from behind dark clouds as Jake drove onto the parking lot of Wheeler's Garage and the place was quiet, no one around, so Jake decided to check the lot for a white Chevy Malibu with mismatched wheels. The lot was gated and padlocked so Jake clambered over the fence, Jake knowing that anything he found would not be admissible in court but wanted confirmation for a direction to take his investigation.

First, he checked the garage entrance which was locked and then looked in the dusty windows where he saw parts scattered on the floor but could not determine if they were from the white Malibu. He strolled to the back lot where several cars in various stages of damage and skeletal husks sat waiting for repair or the elephant boneyard.

It was dark and though Jake didn't like the idea of lighting up his trespass he used a small Maglite to illuminate the vehicles. There were a few white vehicles, but he didn't see the Malibu or anything like it. Dry run.

He walked back to his vehicle and this time shined his light inside the garage and there was a vehicle shape covered by a large tarpaulin. Shining his light on the bottom he could make out the lower edge of the wheels, which were mismatched, but that did not mean this was the Malibu.

Jake moved the light around through the window when a Pit Bull banged against the inside of the window, snarling and growling, which caused Jake to recoil and drop his flashlight.

That was when he felt hands on the backs of his shoulders. Jake twisted the attacker's fingers, turning the man and followed by driving the heel of his hand into the man's ear and neck. Heard a second attacker approach and Jake weaved and dodged to make himself a moving target. Jake kicked at the man's knee, throwing an elbow as he did so, catching the man full in the chest.

More attackers joined the fracas, but Jake could not make out his attackers in the darkness but could make out the forms of three men. He kicked out at the legs of one of the men, was punched in the back of his head and Jake rolled away from the blow as he heard the rush of running as more attackers were closing in.

Jake was trained in Krav Maga but knew his chance at winning against multiple attackers was slim. He could not spend much time on each individual thug but had to do damage and move on to the next man using elbows, knees to attack assailants' eyes, throats, knees, chins, and anything that would discourage their motivation to continue the attack.

Jake lashed out, smashing an elbow against the mouth of a man, kicked out at the shins of another and kept moving so they could not surround him. He felt a jarring thunderbolt at the back of his neck, and he crumpled to the rough ground, unable to move.

They had hit him with a Taser and followed that up with a dose of pepper spray. Jake's body jerked and his eyes burned like acid.

"What the fuck was that?" said a voice.

"You ever see anyone fight like that?" said another faceless man. "He's had training, Richie."

"Motherfucker knocked one of my teeth out, and thanks for using my name, jackass."

Jake was kicked and Richie with the missing tooth said, "Take that, asshole."

"Call the man and ask what we do with this guy."

One man spoke into a phone, but Jake could not hear what was said, and they kept a light shined in his eyes to blind him.

"Shit, it's that cop was here the other day looking for Mickey."

"Boss says take him and his car and take him out and leave him. And hit him with the Taser a few times to teach him not to fuck around." The man leaned down closer to Jake, the light still shining in Jake's eyes and said, "You hear that, Texas boy? We're going to fuck with you some more and you should never come around here again. Be real fucking glad the boss says we don't do cops because you deserve it."

Another man moved in, and Jake smelled the heavy scent of chloroform before he went under.

CHAPTER 33

Jake stirred heavily as the slanting rays of the sunlight hit his face, burning his eyes, and his head buzzed with a sickening twinge as if an alien being was trying to push out the inside of his skull.

Jake was on the bed of his pickup. He rolled and propped up on one elbow and when he tried to sit up a wave of nausea slammed his stomach. He crawled to the rear of the truck bed, leaned over the side and vomited onto the ground. Waves of peristaltic pain trembled inside his stomach and he wretched until he no long had anything to belch out of his damaged body. They had chloroformed him or given him something to knock him out and it was doing a number on his body. He felt like he had been turned inside out. He rolled over on his back and covered his eyes with a forearm and lay that way for several minutes before he heard a tap on the vehicle window.

Jake squinted up at the man with the Medfield PD uniform and said, "Where am I?"

"City Park," said the officer. "We have ordnances against drunks sleeping it off here. Park's closed and you're trespassing."

"I work for Paradise PD and share out with the County as an investigator. I'm Jake Morgan."

"Never heard of you. You got a badge you can show me?"

Jake didn't have his badge with him which wasn't that unusual. He started to chuckle and sucked in his breath when he felt pain in his ribs. "I don't have it."

"Yeah, what a surprise," said the cop. Jake's eyes had adjusted enough that he could read the man's nameplate, 'Dunwoodie'. "Get up, you're going in the drunk tank until I can process you."

Jake held up a hand. "Just call Chief Cal Bannister, Paradise PD or Sheriff Buddy Johnson in Paradise and they'll vouch me. And, I haven't had anything to drink so breathalyze me and you'll know."

"I know both of those men," Dunwoodie said, "So, maybe you're shooting me straight. You look like shit, what the hell happened to you?"

"I got tazed and dosed with pepper spray. And they enjoyed that so much they beat the crap out of me and then forced some nasty shit down my throat."

"'They'. You want to make a report and we'll run them down?"

Jake shook his head and an invisible weasel gnawed at the front of his brain. He moaned and then said, "It was dark, no way I can make a positive ID, plus I was trespassing so they get a pass this time."

But some guy named Richie lost a tooth, so there was a new string to pull.

***

Harper checked her makeup, smoothed her skirt and closed the door to her Jeep. She entered the church where summer's ago she attended Vacation Bible School, her first time in many years as she and her father had attended the First Baptist Church. She felt awkward to attend the funeral of a man she had recently dated without hope of a long-term relationship; as if she had used Jimmy and it made her feel somehow complicit in his tragic end.

But that was silly, wasn't it? But it was there and wouldn't leave her head.

***

It was the church Jake had sat in many Sundays as a young man and it had always made him feel secure and peaceful except for those times when the pastor's message had lighted on a teenager's latest iniquity. Today, it felt lonely and sad.

The church had changed little in ten years. Same wood pews, same carpeting, and the large cross on the wall, softly highlighted by indirect lighting. Sun beams slanted through the arched stained-glass windows and painted rainbow colors on the floor.

Jake had come early and seated himself in a pew towards the back of the sanctuary, hoping to pay his respects to Jimmy Davenport and then quietly slip out before the end of the service. Davenport was dead, murdered before Jake could arrive to help him, and it gnawed at him. He had arrived too late, perturbed that he hadn't pushed Davenport harder early on and felt unworthy to participate in mourning because his position as an investigator cursed him with a detachment from the community where he had gone to school and lived the biggest part of his life. Harper had made him feel attached but that had been severed by circumstance.

It was a separateness he could feel and taste as he sat there. His ribs ached and he could feel the puffiness of a growing black eye.

***

Harper entered the church sanctuary, hushed with thick red carpet runners, white noise and the solemnity of the occasion. She was in heels and wore a two-piece semi-formal outfit with a skirt and jacket. She entered and stood briefly at the back of the church, looking for someone she knew before seating herself and she saw some friends—and Jake Morgan, who had a nasty purple-yellow contusion under his right eye.

***

Jake was thinking about what the next step in his investigation would be, thinking about what Hillary Edson had said about the picture of Judge Preston Carmichael; 'Looked like her father when he was younger', Jake stared at the back of a pew as he considered and didn't notice Harper who now stood next to him until she said, "May I sit here?"

Jake nodded and they sat quietly for a moment. Harper looked at his face and said, "What happened to you."

"Mugged."

"One guy?"

"Four or five."

Harper made a face and said, "Four of five. Why would they do that?"

Jake was considering his response when he felt her take his hand and she softly said, "I'm sorry."

"Yes, it's tough to lose an old friend."

"I'm sorry about that also, Jake," she said.

CHAPTER 34

"Why are we utilizing violence with police officers?" Colin Dukes asked. "Judge Carmichael called and read me the riot act about giving Morgan more incentive to come after this thing."

"Relax," Wheeler said. "He was trespassing and there was no report filed. He couldn't complain as he had no warrant."

"So, this is how they deal with trespassers? Beat the shit out of them. Dammit, Mickey, your guys are stupid."

Wheeler grunted and shrugged, "The boys get a little excited, so what?"

"You know," Dukes said, pointing at Wheeler, "you're in just as much trouble as the rest of us if this investigation continues."

Wheeler wagged a finger at Dukes. "That's not true. See, I don't sample the merchandise; that's for you and your little frat buds. And keep your finger in your pocket when you're talking to me, or I'll be wearing it on a key ring. Does that compute for you, you fuckin' no-dick-havin', uptown boomer?"

Dukes knitted his brow, looked at Wheeler for a long moment, "Who do you think you are, talking to me like that?"

Wheeler gave Dukes a smirking smile and said, "You know who I am and what it means to stay on my good side."

Dukes showed his palms, saying, "Okay, relax, we both have reason to cooperate without rancor. It is just that I would imagine that a low profile would be preferable to stomping a police officer."

"Morgan's on the outs with his cop buddies in Paradise. He's on 'Administrative leave'. They're going to pin this thing on Davenport anyway, so I'm telling you to chill, everything's working out for us."

"So, why are you here, then?"

"Oh yeah," Wheeler said. "There's going to be a change in our business arrangement, you know, overhead, taxes, things like that."

Dukes' teeth ground together, and he said, "You're a fucking blackmailer."

"I prefer 'insurance provider'. Ten percent increase sound good to you, that is, in consideration of recent events?"

"What choice do I have?"

"None."

Hitting up Colin Dukes wasn't Mickey Wheeler's only stop. He also touched base with Frank Jankowski, Senator Stedman, and even Judge Carmichael. One guy he didn't fuck with was the judge's father, Oliver Carmichael, and that one was a different matter. Things were working out for Wheeler in a big way and the death of Jimmy Davenport was a happy consequence as it took the heat off the 'Seek-and-Make' pussies but gave Wheeler an even bigger stick to hold over the heads of the little group of rich kids.

Mickey loved taking the swells over the hurdles, he remembered these guys from school when as a foster kid, they had kept Mickey on the outside of things; Mickey coming to grade school in Salvation Army clothes some other kid had worn before him. Rich kids like Colin Dukes and the jocks like Frank Jankowski laughed at him, but Mickey grew calloused from their abuse and as he grew older and stronger, Mickey turned things around, intimidating the "cool kids" crowd and effecting a tough guy persona that kept them at bay. Mickey had an intelligent organized mind and developed the ability to read people and use that insight to manipulate and control others.

He had gone to school with Dukes, who had once been one of Mickey's tormentors and now Mickey had Dukes by the short hairs. Dukes was his first mark, and Mickey had traded on their "friendship" to make inroads into the rarified air of the Country Club crowd. Dukes introduced Mickey to Senator Stedman which led to Oliver Carmichael and finally to Judge Preston Carmichael, his most valuable chump.

None of them knew that Mickey had something on all of them. And none of them knew of his long con he had manifested that now had taken a lucky turn for Mickey. He had a good idea who had killed the stripper and a better idea who whacked Jimmy Davenport, but it didn't matter.

Thing is, he felt more of a kinship with the cop, Morgan, than any of the assholes he was soaking. Funny to think that way.

Now, maybe there was a way to get Oliver Carmichael on the string, and getting the big dog, the older Carmichael, on a leash could broaden his scope and set up bigger scores. This extortion gig was more lucrative and less gamey than operating a chop shop or running strip clubs.

The problem was that Oliver Carmichael was tougher than his son or his son's buddies and had a longer reach. But Mickey had a plan, and it was working. It had been a long time coming but he had been patient, willing to let it unfold.

The Wild Card was the Texas Ranger, funny he should think of the guy as a Texan when the guy had grown up twenty miles away at Paradise. How'd he miss this guy? Mickey couldn't read Morgan like he could most cops but a lot of what made the guy was right there on the surface and yet there was something smoldering inside like a frozen fire. Most people don't put everything out front, and everyone had an agenda or something to hide.

What Morgan had burning inside was dangerous to his plans.

The dangerous part of Morgan was that he got a kick out of busting bad guys, even enjoyed the give-and-take, which Mickey also enjoyed. That was the connection they had but it could not last.

One of them had to fail and it was going to be Morgan.

CHAPTER 35

Jake was up late going over the crime scene photos and the items Bailey had tagged and documented from her search of Kandy Kane/Cynthia Cross/Sylvia Crane's apartment – phone records, tax documents, while he waited for fingerprint evidence and any DNA not belonging to the victim. In addition, Jake had spent the afternoon running down a birth certificate for Cynthia Cross and now had what he needed or at least hoped he had what he needed. Bailey had done a thorough job of searching and tagging various items and had told him that someone else had gone through the place, probably the killer removing evidence.

"Someone had cleaned up the bathroom and gone through the place. Of course whoever it was will miss some spots so maybe we'll get fingerprints. Medfield PD dusted and provided the prints. The guy was real nice; maybe I'll get a date out of the deal."

Fortunately, Cynthia Cross was a meticulous and organized person who kept receipts, and the room was searched by Bailey who was equally organized and thorough. Two items were of interest; one was a receipt for a pair of earrings like the one Jake found Cynthia was wearing which had Jake thinking about the necklace burn on Cynthia's throat. The killer had started to strangle her with the necklace, but the chain broke and then the killer finished the job with his hands or did the drugs get her first? He looked at the photo of the necklace abrasion closely and then went through the receipts again, couldn't find it.

If the necklace was a gift, did the killer give it to her and then remove it from the crime scene? Would it be possible to ascertain the origin of the necklace from the abrasion pattern? Bailey would know this so he used his cell phone to call the deputy. Bailey sputtered sleepily when she answered his ring.

"What are you doing up, Jake? It's 1:30 in the morning."

"Is there a way to blow up the photo of Cynthia's neck where the necklace burn was, and secondly would I be able to trace the origin, that is, the type and place where the necklace was purchased? I'm guessing the necklace may have been given to her by her killer and that's why he kept it."

"I can blow it up for you and we can look at it and see if that works."

"When?"

"Tomorrow, Jake. Good god, get a life."

The second item that got Jake's attention was a photograph that Jake compared to the photo Meryl Strip had identified as Cynthia's "father". It was a photo Bailey had found in Cynthia's apartment. It was strange that the killer hadn't removed it from the apartment.

"Where'd you find this photo you've tagged as item number 'P' 7A?"

"What does it show?"

"It's a candid, the guy is turned slightly sideways and it's not a great photo, a little fuzzy, as if it was snapped quickly and the man didn't realize he's being photographed."

"Is he wearing a blue baseball cap and sunglasses?"

"That's the one."

"I found it taped to the back of a Monet print, 'Woman with a Parasol'. Unusual for a stripper."

"You think this is a picture of the killer?"

"Maybe. I have another one that may match it. Whether it's the father or the mystery boyfriend I don't know yet. At least it gives me a direction to follow."

"Women select photos and paintings for significance. It makes me sad to think about her looking at the print and imagining a different life."

"Everybody has a dream," Jake said, "Strippers dream, too."

Maybe this stripper dreamed of pointing out her killer.

CHAPTER 36

Morning came and though Jake had only four hours of sleep he was up and energized. Bailey contacted photographer Wiley about enlarging the photos of the necklace abrasions on Cynthia Cross' neck which Bailey thought she recognized as a Brunello Cucinelli chain.

"Those things run about two to three thousand," Bailey said. "That accounts for the unusual abrasion pattern. It's difficult to imagine that it broke as it a series of beaded strands that are corded. The killer must've removed it unless it broke at the clasp."

Bailey provided a photo of the type of necklace she described, and they split up to canvas several jewelry stores in both Paradise and Pinnacle Counties. They didn't find one in any local stores, but Bailey looked it up and learned that it was available at Saks Fifth Avenue on the Country Club Plaza in Kansas City. Jake asked if she would follow up and Bailey told him she would be glad to go shopping on county time.

Officer Dunwoodie of Medfield PD accompanied Jake to Micky Wheeler's garage with the intention of identifying 'Richie', one of Jake's assailants. Jake had checked with Trooper Fred Ridley and asked if he had any run-ins with a guy named 'Richie' who was a known associate of Mickey Wheeler, AKA Mickey Wheels.

Ridley knew Richie and gave Jake good information which allowed him to proceed and get Medfield PD to accompany him in the person of Officer Dunwoodie.

"How are you going to do this?" Dunwoodie asked Jake, as they got out of Dunwoodie's vehicle. "You said it was dark."

"I know his name," Jake said. "And I promise you I can identify him. He's Richie Coleman, his real name is Richie Kohler, and he used to race stock cars on the NASCAR circuit until he got banned, then he worked on pit crews under another false name until somebody found out. Come on, you know you want to do this. How often do you get to take one of Wheeler's guys downtown?"

"We've picked them up before, but nothing sticks."

They walked toward the garage's front door. Dunwoodie wore the dark blue Medfield uniform, and Jake, deciding to be official, was visibly wearing his Paradise County Sheriff's badge. The sun was beaming warm, and gravel crunched under Jake's boots.

"That's because Wheeler has some of your people on the payroll."

Dunwoodie stopped short and looked directly at Jake. "No. No, I don't believe that."

"Well, hell is empty," Jake said, nodding at the garage. "And the devils are here."

"What?" Dunwoodie stopped walking.

"Shakespeare."

Dunwoodie shook his head. "You're a weird guy for a cop. I sure hope this isn't a dry run."

"If you get a complaint from a superior about this bust, you'll know who Wheeler bought off."

Dunwoodie thought about that for a moment, and then nodded his head and said, "You know, shit, you may be right about that."

After the usual preamble of "who are you" and "do you have a warrant" they found Richie Kohler underneath the hood of a late 90's Camaro.

Jake said, "Bet you miss your days on the stock car circuit, worse than you miss the tooth. You know, roaring around the track, being a hero and all."

Richie came up out of the engine compartment and his eyes grew. "Shit, not you, again." Richie had a swollen lip and bruise along his jaw.

"That's the guy," Jake said.

"What's this about a tooth?" Dunwoodie said.

"I knocked it out while he and the other Smurfs were kicking me around."

"Come with us," Dunwoodie said to Richie.

"What'd I do? I didn't do nothing."

"Assault complaint."

"And accessory after the fact to a homicide," Jake said.

"What?"

Mickey Wheeler emerged from his office and said, "What's this about, Dunwoodie?"

Jake waved and said, "We're arresting Richie, assault and homicide accessory."

Wheeler said, "Don't say a fucking word, Richie."

Dunwoodie gave Jake an appraising look and said, "I thought it was about an assault but I'm not sure now."

"Morgan doesn't have jurisdiction here," Wheeler said. "He's suspended. Get the fuck out, Morgan."

"Things aren't always as they appear," Jake said. "I was on 'double-secret fake suspension' and like I told you before, when I'm investigating a homicide I have a lot of latitude and I just kinda bounce around from place to place like a golf ball teed off in a tile bathroom while protecting good citizens like yourself."

"You think everything's funny, don't you?"

"Well, at least this is."

"Dunwoodie, you're shitting in your nest." Wheeler said. "Lieutenant Muswell isn't going to like this."

Jake smiled at Dunwoodie and said, "Told you. Now you know who."

Richie Kohler had priors and happily there was a bench warrant on his alter ego, Richie Coleman, for failure to appear issued by Paradise County on a speeding ticket. Jake dropped the assault charge but invoked the bench warrant and loaded Richie into the back of his Paradise County SUV.

"You know, Richie," Jake said, "this just isn't your day."

"I didn't kill nobody."

"We'll see. Maybe I can get you off the accessory rap if you were to do something like give information I can use."

"I ain't done nothing."

"See, Richie, your problem is you're too dumb to see the big picture. You cheated on the NASCAR circuit, got banned, can't race anymore, and now you're hooked up with one of the area's biggest homicides and you still think you can con your way out of your part. I can put you at the scene of Jimmy Davenport's murder and we'll get your fingerprints for creeping Rufus Crenshaw's place. That was your mistake, or your boss' mistake, trying to find out if Rufus knew anything, and then compounding it by making sure Davenport never talked again. That part pisses me off. Jimmy wasn't a bad guy. Now, I'm sure your employer will drop by with the bail money, and you can tell him that Frank Jankowski has been telling things Wheeler will find interesting."

"Wasn't me did the Davenport dude, man."

"But you know who did?"

"I ain't saying nothing without a lawyer."

"But you did creep Crenshaw's place, tried to intimidate him and you did run from me that night in a White Chevy that was involved in a homicide in Pennsylvania." Jake saw something like surprise in Richie's face. "Didn't know that, did you? I spotted the vehicle the night you and your buddies danced on me, and I got the VIN number. You really should've shipped the car off or burned it."

"How'd you get in the shop?"

Jake hadn't but said, "Professional secret."

It was a lie about the Chevy, but Jake wanted information, even if he just gave Jake another lead to nail down Wheeler's part in the Cynthia Cross homicide. Maybe Wheeler didn't kill the dancer, but Wheeler might know who did and his connection to all the principals involved had something to do with payoffs and extortion because it was what Wheeler did. Mickey Wheels was a scam artist and county crime Lord who bought off high-rollers or blackmailed them. You couldn't buy people like Senator Stedman and Frank Jankowski, and especially not Judge Carmichael, so extortion was Wheeler's leverage.

During his years as a Texas Ranger, Jake learned that criminals usually stayed with what was most effective for them. Small-time C-store robbers robbed C-stores, bank robbers robbed banks, serial killers had a pattern and pimps ran prostitutes. As for Wheeler, despite the fact he was gifted with intelligence and was diversified with the clubs and the chop shop, Jake knew Wheeler's forte was blackmail.

Jake was pretty sure he knew who killed Cynthia Cross, but all he had was circumstantial evidence. He needed more.

"You're up to your ears in this thing, Richie," Jake said. "And I'm going to turn up the heat on you and I'll bet the farm that the people at the top of this thing will be more than happy for you to take the entire weight for the killings which include Davenport and a guy named Adam Driver. So, you gotta decide if you can trust men who gang bang and kill strippers. They have more to hide than you do. You have a nice day, partner."

Jake wanted leverage on Mickey Wheeler and maybe Richie Kohler was the first step, the second step would be when Richie said Jankowski was spilling his guts, which he wasn't, yet.

***

"You're going to be surprised when I tell you who purchased the necklace," Bailey said. Jake was seated at his desk when Bailey walked in. She was wearing off-duty clothing, a green button-down jacket with rolled up sleeves over a lemon-colored blouse and white slacks.

Bailey revealed the name of the man who purchased the necklace and Jake told her he knew that but now it was confirmed. Her mouth fell open and she stared at him for a moment before she said, "Holy shit. How did you know?"

"I haven't been sitting around while you were doing what I would call excellent investigatory work. I spent some time at the hall of records looking at birth certificates. That photo you found in her place along with something Hillary Edson told me about Cynthia Cross' mystery boyfriend, put me on the right track."

"So why was she killed?"

"The motive is still elusive, yet I have one and pretty sure if I play it right, a couple of the men involved will tell me what I want to know. I'm going to play them against each other and let them think this is the only way they don't end up in Jefferson City for the remainder of their lives."

"I'll never understand you, Jake. C'mon, tell me what you're up to."

"Patience, Bailey, patience. I'm not sure of my thesis and Sherlock Holmes cautions against twisting evidence to support your theory."

"Sherlock Holmes? Where are you getting this?"

"From that poet-warrior football coach, Leo the Lion."

CHAPTER 37

"I just bailed Richie," Mickey Wheeler said. "And Richie says Jankowski is talking to the cops. Better get Langley over there and shut him up."

"Why do you imagine I have thoughts about your employee's predicament, Mr. Wheeler?" Oliver Carmichael said. "And why would I waste Langley on him?"

"Because your son, the judge, is involved and that makes you involved. I know you're the guy who told him about the girl, you know, Cynthia Cross. I've got a photocopied birth certificate that will pucker up your sphincter. That's right, Ollie. I know about your relationship to Cynthia Cross, and you should be careful about pissing me off."

"Don't threaten me, Wheeler. I don't do well with threats."

"I ain't making a threat, I'm warning you of the consequences of inaction. I'm not your problem. Your problem is about your dick and your son's dick and that fucking sheriff's bloodhound, Morgan, is all over this and right now, Frank Jankowski is talking. You want this shut down, you'll do what I'm telling you."

"And then what next?"

"You know what's next. I shouldn't have to say it and I'm not going to. Nothing to me either way, but your son is on the railroad tracks and a train's coming."

As Jake expected and halfway hoped, Charles Langley was the attorney of record for Richie Kohler.

"Charles Langley representing a guy like Richie?" Buddy Johnson said, when Langley asked to see his client. "That's incredible."

"It is, isn't it?" Jake said.

"This thing is coming together but I don't see yet how we tie it up and connect it to the homicide. I mean, I see what you're doing and I would applaud it if it didn't swell your head up more than it already is, but these are people with the power to pull this off right in our faces and walk. The evidence will have to be unassailable, and we need someone to talk to us."

"We don't have much on Richie Kohler, almost nothing really, but the fact that Langley showed tells me we're on the right track. And Richie knows more than he's telling, and they will either have to shut him up, one way or another. I planted a seed of doubt with Richie that I hope will gnaw away at his trust for his compatriots. I dropped a dime on Frank Jankowski that he is talking – a bluff but I'll turn over that card today."

"Now what?" Buddy asked.

"We fingerprinted and swabbed Richie and we see if Zeke the Sheik can match him to anything in Jimmy Davenport's place and squeeze him some more or, for better or worse, maybe they'll disappear Richie somehow. I'm going to visit Jankowski about a possible assault charge on an exotic dancer named Meryl Strip, real name Hillary Edson. Jankowski will either bluster and hedge or he will start selling out the other guys. As for Richie, I learned why he was banned from NASCAR."

"He was a NASCAR driver? Good work, Jake."

"Richie didn't qualify for the Daytona Coke Zero Sugar 400. He just missed qualifying by one car. There was a fire that burned up the #35 qualifier car and Richie made the cut. Thing is, the driver of the #35 qualifier was badly burned in the fire while trying to put it out. NASCAR officials and the police couldn't prosecute

Richie and had to let him race but when Richie ran another racer into the wall at his next race, NASCAR went ahead and banned him. Richie is pretty capable of murder, but he didn't kill Cynthia Cross."

"How do you know that?"

"He had no reason and wasn't tied to her homicide until after she was killed. I do think he was the instrument they're using to shut people up, like Adam Driver and Davenport."

"All right, Jake, I know you and bet you know who killed the Cross girl. Who are you thinking?"

"Sit down, Buddy. Langley showing up confirms what I surmised. We need to go see Darcy Hillman and get her to issue warrants for homicide and accessory after the fact of the homicide. You're not going to believe this even if I tell you, but I have the evidence and I know what went down."

CHAPTER 38

Perfect irony was what Jake would call it later. Jake caught up with Frank Jankowski's golf cart on the 18th hole, chatting up a beer cart girl, a brunette not much older than Jankowski's daughter. Jankowski was leaning in on her car, eyeing her, so intent on his appraisal he didn't notice Jake until he was close by.

"What're you doing here, Morgan?"

"Frank, we need to talk. You have information I want and you're going to be happy to give it to me."

"Get lost. I don't want to talk to you."

"Young lady," Jake said, addressing the girl. "I think you need to leave us."

The girl was apprehensive, her eyes moving from Jake to Jankowski and back to Jake again.

"Be careful," Jake said. "He hurts little girls like you."

"What's going on here, Mr. Jankowski?" the girl said.

"Ignore him," Jankowski said, bristling now. "He's nobody."

"I could show her my badge, you like."

Jankowski glowered some more before he said, "Go on, Beth, we'll talk later."

"I have to get going anyway," Beth said. She engaged the cart and got moving.

Jankowski watched her drive off and without looking at Jake he said, "I'm still not going to talk to your dumbass."

"Then you're under arrest for assault."

"What? Bullshit."

"Her name's Meryl Strip, real name is Hillary, but you wouldn't know that would you, you creepy girl-hitting has been?"

Jankowski took a step towards Jake and drew up to his full size. "I oughta kick your ass."

"What if you can't do that? I'm not a girl or a stripper."

"If you didn't have that badge, I'd pound you like a nail."

Jake took his badge out of his pocket, placed it on Jankowski's cart and said, "There. Where do you want to do this? Right here where everyone can see it? Or do we go behind the caretaker's shed? And, I gotta tell you something, Frank, I really don't like guys who beat up women. I got a thing about it so I'm looking forward to putting you on the other end of it."

Jankowski's eyes darted about, to see if anyone was looking.

"What is it you want?"

"Well, besides the assault charge, I'm here to place you under protective custody."

"Protect me from who?"

"Your buddies in Seek-and-make. Somebody told them you were ready to give testimony in exchange for immunity in the Cynthia Cross homicide."

"Who did that?"

"Me."

"They won't believe that."

"I don't know, I laid it on pretty thick. Let me give you a couple names they thought were going to talk. Try Jimmy Davenport and Adam Driver. They're both dead. How's that? Not too late for immunity, Frank. First one in is the only guy we'll listen to, but I do have one other on the string. Your call."

CHAPTER 39

Jake was hungry and realized he hadn't sat down to eat in the past 18 hours, so he met Harper for lunch at the Dinner Bell.

"You might want to take a breath now and then," Harper said, as Jake devoured his Bacon Cheeseburger. Harper had her hair pulled back and she smell like a summer morning with the promise of a better day. "When's the last time you ate?"

"I'm close on the thing I've been working on."

"Jimmy didn't do it?"

Jake took two French fries in his hand and said, "I never thought he did, the real killer or killers fed Davenport to the media to take the heat off."

"Killers? Plural? There's more than one?"

Jake ate the French fries and held up a hand while he chewed before saying, "No, the actual homicide was by one man but there are others involved who may not know they're involved but were part of the club party that involved a gang-rape and therefore are accessories after the fact and they may not have any choice but to ride it out."

"And who would that be?"

Jake started to pick up another fry and said, "That's all I can give you right now."

"What happened to 'trust you more than anyone'?"

Jake closed one eye and screwed up his face before

he said, "You should've been a cop yourself."

She sighed, put an elbow on the table and leaned her chin down on her palm and said, "Why? Between Dad and Buddy, I hear all the cop stuff I need."

"I got Rufus off on the DUI, that is, he's not going to jail, but he still has to pay a fine and lose points on his license."

"Thank you."

"If you really wanted to thank me –"

"Slow down, dummy. We're not quite there yet."

"Yet, sounds 'imminent'."

She closed her eyes, smiled and shook her head. "No one can say you're not an optimist. Now, you need to work on being a realist."

"Okay, I'll tell you tomorrow night when I take you out to dinner."

"What makes you assume that I will go out to dinner with you?" Harper said, her blue eyes merry with amusement.

"Because first, you're a cop's daughter who wants to know how it ends and second because you're in love with me and it's time to stop driving each other crazy. When you're my wife you'll get to know all the good stuff going on."

"Boy, that's a leap," she said, laughing to herself. "You're arrogant and kind of a jackass so what makes you think I'd marry you?"

"So, what's your answer?"

Shaking her head now. "I want a church wedding and I want to honeymoon in Hawaii."

"Hawaii? So yes, right?"

"The answer was always going to be yes, dummy."

CHAPTER 40

Jake showered, shaved while Tchaikovsky's Symphony number 6 in B minor swelled and surged to its climax. Jake was at the end of a tumultuous morning of police work and now he was about to realize the fruition of his investigation.

Darcy Hillman balked at issuing the requested warrants until Jake and Buddy laid things out and assuaged her reluctance. The depositions from Frank Jankowski and Dr. Drake Thurgood along with a birth certificate Jake had uncovered did the trick.

Richie Kohler was now willing to flip on his benefactors in return for a reduced sentence, but would not turn on Mickey Wheels, which demonstrated to Jake that Wheeler was more to be feared than a sitting judge and a state senator. Something to remember.

Jake wanted to get all of them but at a loss how to get Wheeler unless someone turned on the man.

"Good luck if you can make this stand up in court," Darcy said. "And we're all screwed if it doesn't. Working with you two, especially you, Morgan, is a high wire act with no net." She handed the documents to Buddy who would then pass them off to his deputies for serving them. "All right here they are."

"These warrants have to be issued in coordination," Buddy said. "I will instruct my team to hit all the principles at the same hour and we will postpone any public announcement of arrests until Jake can confront our final suspects and finish this off. Agreed?"

With the assistance of Paradise County Deputies Bailey and Makepeace along with assistance from Trooper Fred Ridley, Frank Jankowski, Senator Wyck Stedman, Dr. Drake Thurgood, Colin Dukes and Judge Preston Carmichael would be served warrants and arrested at 8:30 AM. Thurgood and Jankowski's arrest were to protect them from reprisal from the others. All were charged with 'accessory after the fact' and would be forced to submit to DNA sampling. Maybe nothing would stick but Jake needed them rounded up when he went after the big dog, Judge Preston Carmichael. Mickey Wheels was not involved in the round-up.

"I'm hoping that Carmichael will give up Mickey Wheels and fill in the blanks about Cynthia Cross," Jake said.

"What're your thoughts on that?" Ridley asked.

"I want to know when did Carmichael learn that Cynthia Cross was his half-sister and who told him."

Jake and Ridley arrived to detain Preston Carmichael for the murder of Cynthia Cross and produced the warrant to Carmichael's secretary who placed a hand to her mouth, let out a small moan and said, "Oh my god, I don't believe this, let me call him." She tried the intercom but there was no answer. "He is here though."

Jake and Ridley entered the office, they discovered the lifeless body of Judge Preston Carmichael, face down on the floor by his desk chair. There were some yellow capsules strewn on his desk.

When Dr. Ezekial Montooth arrived, he looked at the corpse, noted a frothy pinkish spittle on Carmichael's lips and also at the yellow capsules. "There is no signs of violence, no damage to the body. My preliminary thought is that this is suicide by Nembutal overdose."

"He knew we were coming," Ridley said. "So much for anything we'll learn from him."

Jake scratched his forehead and said, "Well, I have one

more person we can push, and I have something that may motivate him to assist us."

***

"All this searching, all this work and now I'm here," Jake said. He wore his Texas Ranger dress shirt, black cherry Lucchese boots and his Paradise County Sheriff's badge clipped to his belt. Trooper Fred Ridley was razor sharp in his Highway Patrol Blues, pressed and starched, his Smokey the Bear hat on his lap. "I'm wanting to resolve this thing, you know, clear up the loose ends and I could certainly use your help and influence."

Jake and Ridley were in the office of the big man himself, the man who had inadvertently set the wheels in motion for the murder of Cynthia Cross years before.

"How can I help you, Mr. Morgan?" Oliver Carmichael said, giving Jake the big smile and shaking his hand.

"Thank you for receiving us today, I realize you're a busy man. This involves a homicide case I'm working; you may have heard of it. Her name was Cynthia Cross. She was raped, murdered and discarded in a ditch on a country road."

"Not familiar with the name."

Jake lifted his chin a half-inch and raised his eyes, as if thinking about it, before saying, "Her mother's name is Sylvia Crane and I believe you do know her and know her well."

The smile ran away from Oliver's face.

"Whoops, that one hit home, didn't it?" Jake felt good now as he turned things around. "I have Dr. Drake Thurgood and Frank Jankowski under deposition. Turns out Dr. Thurgood was working with both your son and the deceased, Cynthia Cross, and whether intentionally or inadvertently, somehow your son, Preston, learned that his lover was also his half-sister. That, or you revealed it when you could not stomach the thought of this incestuous –"

Oliver Carmichael interrupted Jake. "This is preposterous and insulting. You come into my office under false pretenses..." The older man paused, recovered and then said, "Do you know who I am?"

"Yeah, you're the guy that had sex with a woman just over twenty years ago who gave birth to your daughter, Cynthia Cross. You didn't know about Cynthia until years later. I don't know who revealed that your son was having a sexual affair with his half-sister. To your credit you set up Cynthia with a nice apartment, and tried to make up for your mistake, or as some would say, your sin, by becoming her benefactor if you could not act as her father. But the alternate explanation for your largesse would be that you or your son was being blackmailed."

"You have no proof of any of this."

"Oh yeah, I forgot." Jake opened a binder and produced and held up a document. "I have a document here, a birth certificate and a deathbed statement from a Mr. Ralph Philpott stating that," Jake held up the paper and began reading, "I have been receiving cash payments for the lease of Miss Sylvia Crane from—" Jake halted reading and looked up at Oliver Carmichael. "Should I say the name?"

Oliver Preston rocked back-and-forth in the high-backed leather chair. "This is ridiculous. I'll have your badge. I'll have you ruined."

"I don't think so, Ollie. I think this will pretty much ruin you once it hits the media, not to mention what it's going to do to your son's legacy."

Oliver Carmichael held up a hand and said, "Wait. Just slow down, sir. We can work something out to our mutual benefit. I can help you immensely. You're a sharp young man; how would you feel about a position with the FBI?"

Jake shook his head. "Mr. Carmichael, I was a Texas Ranger and chose to serve Paradise County, why would a Texas Ranger lower himself to work with bureaucrats?" Jake stood. "Let's get something straight. I don't like you and the way you do things."

"Get out of my office."

"Looking into court documents I learned that your son, Judge Carmichael, made a sweetheart deal on a homicide beef for Richie Kohler. Richie Kohler killed Jimmy Davenport, and Richie is right now talking to Paradise County PA Hillman and it's like he's never going to stop talking and your name keeps coming up. I have deputies standing by with a warrant for your complicity in the solicitation to commit murder by proxy which I believe will stick and even if it doesn't, you're done."

Oliver Carmichael wiped his mouth with a hand and became more agitated.

"I have some bad news," Jake said. "This morning, your son, Judge Preston Carmichael, committed suicide due to the fact that he murdered his half-sister and knew we were coming to arrest him. I have DNA evidence to support this position, despite the judge moving the body and Charles Langley's attempts to prevent me from interviewing these men. I have enough to bring this to a grand jury and Preston's suicide will not stop that. In a way, this is your fault, sir."

Oliver's face reddened, he began to exhale with his mouth open, and his eyes widened like a frightened horse. He held up a hand and said, "Wait. Though you are right about some things I did not hire the person you mention. If you –." Oliver paused, produced a handkerchief, and mopped his brow. "If you will allow me to contact my attorney, I will give you a statement that may help you."

Jake looked at Ridley, Ridley nodded, and Jake nodded and said, "You may call Mr. Langley."

CHAPTER 41

Jake commandeered Oliver Carmichael's desk where he sat rolling a quarter over the back of his fingers. Ridley lifted his eyes to the ceiling in amused disbelief at Jake's antics, while Oliver Carmichael sat in a chair facing his own desk. Charles Langley of Langley, Pope and Hardy was incensed.

"You deliberately attempted to push Oliver into a heart attack," Langley said. "We will be filing a suit for harassment and wrongful prosecution."

Jake watched the quarter flip and roll over his fingers for a moment, stopped, rubbed his eyes and said, "I can't wait until we get to the discovery portion. Ollie's going to love you when I drop the big one."

"Charles," Oliver said, "that is not the way we are going to proceed. Did you bring the documentation I requested?"

"Of course I did, Oliver." Langley turned his head sideways and considered Jake from the corner of his eyes. "What do you mean the big one?"

"Cynthia Cross was Oliver's illegitimate child and that his son, Preston, was having a sexual affair with Cynthia. Dr. Thurgood, Rufus Crenshaw, Lanny Wannamaker will all testify that your other clients, Wyck Stedman and Frank Jankowski were present the night of the murder. I have a star witness, Richie Kohler, who in return for a lighter sentence confessed to the murder of Jimmy Davenport and that he was hired by both Carmichaels to kill Davenport." Jake leaned back in his chair, and said, "So, Chuck, you just do your best and I will spend a couple of days on the stand testifying to the many reasons for our interest in all your clients."

Langley was quiet for several moments, placed a finger on his lips and then said, "How about we work out a compromise on these charges. You've already got a full sack, as it were, we ought to be able to do something to lessen the damage to my clients."

"I'm an all-or-nothing kinda guy and you're stuck with me."

Langley pursed his lips, thought some more, looked at his client and said, "Oliver?"

Oliver's shoulders sagged and he looked deflated. "My son is dead as is my daughter. Gentleman, may I consult with my attorney before I give you my decision?"

"I think that would be best," Ridley said.

Jake and Ridley left the office. Outside, Ridley said, "What if he chooses to say nothing?"

"Then we're no worse off than when we got here."

Ten minutes passed and the door opened, and Langley motioned them back into the office.

Langley did the talking, while Oliver Carmichael, the kingmaker and giant of Missouri politics sat, his Rep tie open and dangling, staring at the floor and breathing through his mouth.

"Mr. Carmichael does not wish to have his son's name trumpeted through the press and feels it will serve no purpose. He has information that may help you."

"'May help' is too thin," Jake said. "He will have to give me what I want."

"He asks that Stedman be granted immunity from prosecution."

"No. Stedman is a dirty politician who may have been involved in the death of a coed many years ago and used his office to have it declared an accidental drowning. I believe, though I have no evidence, that Preston was also involved in that. I will make sure that gets known."

"Perhaps if Stedman would withdraw from consideration for the U.S. Senator's race."

"Still no."

Langley paused, took a breath, and turned his attention to Oliver.

Oliver Carmichael closed his eyes and nodded his head.

Langley looked at Jake for a long moment before he said, "We can give you Mickey Wheeler."

"Charley," Jake said. "That's music to my ears."

CHAPTER 42

Langley looked at the beaten Oliver Carmichael who nodded his acceptance. The non-verbal communication between political fixer and high-powered attorney was a sentient one that possessed a long and symbiotic relationship and the reason for the rise of both men in their chosen fields.

Oliver said, "I would like to have a drink before I begin."

"Okay with me," Jake said. "Ridley?"

"Sure."

Without a word, Langley rose from his seat and walked to a cabinet, looked back at his long-time associate and said, "The good stuff?"

Oliver nodded and Langley produced a bottle of Pappy Van Winkle, held up the bottle and asked, "Gentlemen, would you like a taste? 15 years old."

Ridley said, "I'm on duty."

Jake said, "Pappy Van Winkle? Almost worth getting fired, but just almost."

Oliver Carmichael had quite a story to tell and Jake shared it with Darcy Hillman and Sheriff Buddy Johnson in the PA's office. Jake wanted a warrant for Wheeler, and Trooper Ridley was in attendance to confirm Jake's story.

"It boils down to the fact that highly intelligent and

savvy people had underestimated the cunning and intellect of Mickey 'Wheels' Wheeler. Wheeler had Colin Dukes under his thumb because Dukes had strange sexual tastes, same with Jankowski. Wheeler's mistake was over-reach when he attempted to pull the political giant, Oliver Carmichael, into his blackmail net.

When Oliver learned of his daughter's existence, he moved to accommodate her needs. However, Cynthia Cross revealed this information to Wheeler and the pair began to work Judge Carmichael using Cross' alter ego, Kandy Kane, to seduce the judge. Judge Preston Carmichael did not know Cynthia was his sister until shortly before he killed her though Cynthia was aware of the fact."

Buddy said, "So, Wheeler blackmailed the judge for his affair with his sister?"

"At first, Wheeler blackmailed the judge for his affair with Cross not knowing she was the sister," Jake said. "Judge Carmichael was not eager for his wife and children to learn of the affair. When Wheeler learned Cross and the judge were brother and sister he decided to extort money from Carmichael's father. The older Carmichael could not stand it and told his son, which greatly distressed Preston, who then angrily confronted Wheeler, telling him he was no longer going to pay the extortion money."

"That was a bold move by Preston," Hillman said. "That had to be gut-wrenching."

Jake nodded. "It was. Wheeler, being who he is, decided to get revenge on the judge for breaking their arrangement, and brought Kandy Kane to the gang-bang at the Country Club. The shrink, Dr. Thurgood, told me that when Cynthia arrived at the Country Club she was killed, Judge Carmichael was visibly shaken and flew into a rage when his half-sister showed up for the strip show."

"Oliver Carmichael was troubled by the suicide and murder, but neither concerned him as much as the incest," Ridley said.

"And how it is tied to Oliver, of course," Hillman said. "This is some twisted stuff."

"Judge Carmichael, in the heat of rage, killed her. He tried to strangle her with a necklace he had bought for her but finished by choking her to death with his bare hands, then keeping the necklace, which was a mistake. He told no one in the group which made each member suspicious of the others."

Buddy broke in and said, "Davenport came back to lock up and saw Cynthia Cross leave with the judge which is the reason Davenport was killed."

"Yeah," Jake said. "Adam Driver must've also seen that, but we may never know who killed him though my money is on Wheeler who likes the street cred as a killer."

"So, Jimmy was not involved in the murder?" Buddy said. "That's a relief. He wasn't a bad guy."

"No, but he was involved in the gang-rape as part of his initiation into the group which is the way the mafia enslaves their people," Ridley said. "The sexual act was akin to Davenport 'making his bones'."

"Wheeler was smart," Jake said. "His extortion industry was guaranteed cash flow for him and gave him political juice. Wheeler didn't want Judge Carmichael named as the killer as that would dry up a source of blackmail money, so he had Richie kill Davenport and probably Driver. With Adam Carmichael's deposition we've got Wheeler for extortion, and I believe Richie will flip and give us Wheeler for Davenport's homicide."

Jake stopped and said, "Is that enough?"

Darcy signed the papers and handed them to Jake. "Go get him."

CHAPTER 43

Trooper Ridley and Medfield PD officer Dunwoodie accompanied Jake to arrest Mickey Wheeler. Ridley and Dunwoodie detained Wheeler's employees while Jake issued his warrant.

Jake slid into Wheeler's office, weapon drawn, and announced to a surprised Wheeler, that he was "under arrest for extortion and conspiracy for murder of Jimmy Davenport".

Wheeler folded his arms over his chest, smirked and said, "You'll have a hell of a time proving that."

The Kimber .45 was out and on Wheeler's desk, close enough to Wheeler to grab it quickly which told Jake Wheeler was expecting them. Jake's first thought was to control the situation and confiscate the weapon, but he had a different idea.

"You'll get your chance in court," Jake said. "Oh wait, I forget to tell you, Charles Langley has withdrawn from your defense team and Richie is spilling his guts. Guess you'll have to hire some local attorney. I'll bet there's a bidding war for that and just as your extortion money dries up. Tough luck, Wheels."

Wheeler looked at Jake with hooded eyes now, the smug look had left his face. Wheeler said, "Guess this is better than a showdown between us, for you. You have your gun drawn and a warrant. It would've been better if you'd cornered me in an alley and we could've settled this. I would've loved to see you make good on your threat to make me eat my piece."

Jake smiled, and said, "Okay, go for it."

"What?"

"It's right there in front of you. Go ahead, I'm not kidding." Jake holstered his SIG Sauer and said, "Okay, Wheels, make your play."

"You are fucking crazy. You want a Wild West showdown with cops just outside?"

"I've been amused by your smooth criminal act and killing two men which you alluded to that first time I was here. 'Not with this gun' you said. Now, you have your chance to show me what a stone-killer you are."

"I do that, I'll go to prison."

Jake hardened his look and said, "You're going anyway, I've got you cold. Now, you talk tough, and here's your chance, but you're a back-shooting chickenshit who never faced anybody down in your life. I have, more than once and even lately. So, in the immortal words of Josey Wales, 'Are you gonna draw that pistol or whistle Dixie'?"

Wheeler eyed the Kimber, then gritted his teeth and glared at Jake. "You prick, I ought to—"

Wheeler's right shoulder twitched, and he started to reach for the weapon, but he stopped himself and exhaled.

Jake reached out and picked up the weapon.

"What I thought," Jake said. "You have the right to remain silent, anything you say can and will be used against you in a court of law..."

MAXXED AGAIN:
A COLE SPRINGER NOVELLA

by W. L. RIPLEY

CHAPTER 1

Cole Springer's first incident as a Secret Service agent in the Presidential detail probably started the ball rolling.

Well, at least the first one made the second one inevitable, which led to other things.

Springer was standing outside a hotel room, a really nice hotel, in Germany while the President was inside the room with a lady not his wife. You knew his wife you could understand it but still, it was shit detail, pretending you were doing something to safeguard America.

But, that was the secret service. You did what they said and you went where the President went within certain limits.

The first incident, yeah. He was standing there minding his own business, guarding the most powerful man in the world and a couple of Washington Post guys found out where he was staying. Well, he wasn't staying in that room exactly, he was staying three floors up but the guy always checked into two rooms wherever he stayed or would commandeer one of the SS guy's rooms for his "meetings".

This time he had chosen Springer's room which didn't sit well but how do you tell the President sorry sir, I don't want your biological stains on my bed, thank you anyway and the guy, who Springer hadn't voted for in the first place, didn't even ask permission.

Anyway, he's standing outside the room, *Springer's* personal room, guarding the door thinking maybe he really should've pursued the baseball thing when these two half-in-the-bag journalists, tell Springer they want to talk to the President.

"He's not in there," Springer said.

"Then why are you guarding the door?"

Well they had him there.

"Free cocktails down the hall, help yourself," he told them

"C'mon, man. He's in there. Ask him if we can talk to him."

"No."

Drunk reporter number one says, "I hear the POTUS is a pussy-hound. That true?"

The other SS man, Mike McCall, a guy Springer liked working with said, "You guys need to move along."

Drunk reporter #2 said, "Does he have a woman in there?"

Springer didn't change expression and said, "You're the reporter, what do you think he's doing?"

They all laughed and the two reporters went looking for more free drinks. McCall saying, after they left, "Man you shouldn't have said that, Cole."

Springer shrugged. "I couldn't resist."

Which led to incident number two with the god-almighty Secretary of State.

"Are you fucking stupid?" is what the Secretary, a large man with a beef-and-bourbon face. "You don't give those journalist's anything to extrapolate."

"'Extrapolate'? Wow. I should look that word up, right?"

"You know Springer, your mouth gets you in trouble with me and gets all of us in trouble with the media, who enjoy your wiseass attitude, an attitude that creates more work trying to explain away what you're saying to they don't get the wrong impression."

"What was I saying?" said Springer, looking straight

ahead.

"You intimated that there was a woman in the room."

"Actually it wasn't an intimation as much as it was a question."

Springer could see the little veins building in the guy's forehead.

"Shut up, Springer."

"Yes sir," said Springer. "Immediately."

Which also kind of set the guy off. Not the 'yes sir' so much as the little pause before he added, 'immediately', and maybe the faint smile.

"You know, you think you're special, Springer. You're a Goddamn smartass and we don't need smartasses in this detail. You're protecting the leader of the free world and you think it's the fucking Comedy Channel. It's an important, no critical, detail. Look at me when I'm talking to you, Springer."

So he did. He looked at the Secretary of State. But, that didn't make the man happy because maybe the amused look on Springer's face.

"Let me tell you something else—what are you smiling about?"

"Sometimes I smile so hard inwardly at the caprices of life that it shows on the outside."

Which lit the fuse. The Secretary was a step away from jumping up and down and frothing at the mouth, spittle forming and Springer knew that he was down a road with no turn around.

"The President likes you, Springer, or you would already be gone. Personally, I don't like your attitude and I don't like you."

"Well, I really like you sir." He didn't. "And I'm devastated to learn of your feelings."

"Don't patronize me."

"Sure."

"Don't keep smarting off."

"I'd just have to keep explaining myself and I'd get tired of it."

And now they had reached the yelling spitting phase of

the discussion which was *did Springer know who he was talking to, did Springer know how the man could ass-fuck his life,* and *Springer was one step away from a detail guarding polar bears at the Arctic Circle when...*

The spittle forming on the corner of the Secretary's mouth landed on Springer's face.

Springer felt the spit, reaching up with one hand and wiping it from his face, looking full-on into the Secretary's face. The man stopped yelling for a moment just before Springer said:

"Don't spit on me."

"You deserve it." The Secretary said.

Very calmly, without any rancor, Cole Springer of the Secret Service said, "How about I fix it so you sneeze in your ear?"

End of that career.

There were other incidents, scenarios, moments in his SS career that had led up to this defining moment.

So, Springer cashed in his pension money and bought some land in Colorado to open a bar. He bought the bar from Max Shapiro, a mob money-launderer, who gave him a good price. But the land was located in a red-zone. A red zone being a fly over for jumbo jets and other loud noises.

That had been his first exposure to Max Shapiro which led to Springer protecting him from one of the Rocky Mountains nastiest underworld bosses, Nicky Tortino, by faking Max's death and then getting Max to roll over on Tortino with the FBI and that led to Max being placed in the Federal Witness Protection.

However...

CHAPTER 2

Max didn't like the witness protection program. That was the first thing Max said, when he called Springer and before Springer could say anything Max said, "You think you'd like it? Living in a ranch house with a sod lawn in Backwards, Arkansas. Eating frozen TV dinners that give me heartburn and breakfast at McDonald's, the only restaurant in town without broken down chairs. I ask the local grocer to lay in some smoked Salmon and he looked at me like I was growing a second nose."

It was raining lightly and Cole Springer was sitting in his deck hot tub when the call came. His shoulder, an old baseball injury was hurting, and he wanted to whirlpool it. Classic Max Shapiro. He always had a complaint. Springer smiled thinking about Max in Arkansas. Max had been a mob money launderer and a real estate speculator. Max was rich, very rich. Max was also a pain-in-the-ass who was always whining about something. But, Springer had to give it to Max, the guy knew how to turn a buck.

"They sent you to Arkansas? Somebody has a sense of humor."

"It's in a dry county, you can believe it? I gotta drive 30 miles to buy a bottle of Scotch or join one of their "clubs" which is some back room with a hog's head on the wall. These yeehaw morons fuck domestic animals or something. You should see the place."

"It's a mistake to come out in the open, you know that. They'll find you."

"That? Aw, hell, they forgot all about that. I'm working for 'em again. Working for Sonny Blue. I'm good at it, you know that. Besides, Nicky T was killed last year. He was the only guy after me. Some kind of professional hit."

Springer knew who killed Nicky Tortino and then tried to whack Springer also but kept it to himself.

"I thought you didn't want to work with them anymore."

"That's because I was dying...thought I was dying. When you know you're going to be around next month you get a different perspective about who you work with. It ain't so bad. I make good money, eat in good restaurants, and date a showgirl now and then."

"What about Suzi?"

There was a pause on the line. He knew that would twist Max up and Springer did it on purpose. Max was fun to piss off.

"You know about Suzi, you lowlife. You palmed her off on Gerry Nugent."

"You were screwing that up all by yourself."

"Yeah, well. I bought you a plane ticket. It's in your name at Aspen airport."

This was like Max, assuming you would do what he wanted, not bothering to ask. He was spoiled that way.

"Max, I'm not coming out there. You got yourself in trouble, get yourself out. So they sent you to Arkansas, huh? I love it. Go to Fayetteville and catch a Razorback game."

"I left there. I'm in Vegas, which is why the feds got their undies in a bunch."

"I don't Vegas and I got things to do."

"Like spend my fucking money."

"Also that," Springer said. "Thank you."

"See, I'm forgetting how hard you are to talk to. Like you think it's some type of comedy routine. You know I'll pay."

"I've got money."

"Yeah, you blew mine up to get it."

"You're alive aren't you? You sure don't have much appreciation, me saving your life and all. I could've walked away, let them have you."

"Except you wanted the money. So, don't come off like you're Gary Cooper doing favors. Saving me was incidental to you getting your hands on that money."

There was no use going on with Max. Cole either had to hang up or ask what kind of trouble he was in. Remembering how much trouble Max could get into and there was the fact that he really kind of like Max, so Springer decided to ask about the trouble.

Max said, "It's like this. I got this friend. He's from back east. I vouch him on a private game then he loses big and skips."

"I'm not surprised he's a friend of yours."

"Yeah, hahaha, you're funnier than sandpaper condom, you know that? Why do you feel moved to comment? Why don't you just listen, huh? Oy. Anyway, he skipped and now the guys are coming after me for what he owes."

"So, pay it, money's not your problem."

"They don't want just money."

"Yeah, what do they want?"

"They want a finger. Yeah, that's right. That's what these sick fucks want. It's like being in a bad movie, these guys always coming up with new ways to jerk each other off. Anyway, they've been sending around these two ogres, looking like a failed lab experiment to ask me where my friend is."

"Where is your friend?"

"What do you think I need you for? Aren't you listening? I knew where he was, I'd cut his fucking finger off myself and bring it wrapped in bacon, the goy bastard."

"Always a lyrical way of putting things." He looked at the timer on the hot tub. Couple more minutes. He'd be dripping all over the carpet when he got inside or if he went through the other door, it was hardwood floor and taking a chance on slipping and falling down. Bad either way, but you had to choose.

"Come on, take the ticket and come get me, Springer. You can't leave me out here with these animals."

"Oh, I can."

"They'll take one of my balls off with a pair of linemen's pliers and laugh about it. Yeah, that's how they are. Ghouls."

"There's people there that hire out for that."

"I've asked around but nobody wants to buck these guys." There was another pause and he could hear noise like Max was working up to something.

"Who do these guys work for?"

"You're going to like this part. It's a friend of yours, Red Cavanaugh."

Springer shook his head. Only Max could get himself in a mix like this with a sadistic crazy like Red Cavanaugh. But, now Springer was intrigued. Red Cavanaugh. Really?

"Cavanaugh sort of dislikes me, you know."

Max said, "I'm hearing that."

Springer thinking that Max is in trouble with one of the nastiest loan sharks west of the Rockies and can still think it's funny that Cavanaugh hates Springer. Then, Max said, "Much as I hate to give you anything that'll swell your head up any more than it is, the fact is, you're honest. You say you're gonna do something, it gets done. And, you're not afraid of these guys."

"I don't know where you get the idea I'm not afraid of those people. Red Cavanaugh would have me shot with as much moral ambiguity as eating a ham sandwich. I'm sitting in a hot tub in the Rockies with a beer beside me and you want me to come out there and sweat and dodge Red Cavanaugh? Your thought processes amaze me."

"Well, there's something you have to do first."

"What's that?"

"Come get me out of here. They've got me boxed in. I can't leave my place they're not in my face. I don't produce the guy by next week they're going to take my finger instead."

"Aw, Max..."

"And bring some money too."

"Why do I need to bring money?"

"I'm a little short right now. You ever run short?"

Springer said, "How much?"

Max made a dismissive noise in his throat at the other end of the line. "Not much. Maybe three."

"Three what? Thousand?"

"Are you kidding? I strike you as somebody can't generate three grand? I carry that much around. The fucking feds got my assets frozen because they're pissed at me for jumping witness protection."

"How much?"

"Okay, Three Hundred Thousand."

Springer said, "Why do I get the feeling your buddy owes that much?"

"You'll get it back when I move some stuff around. You wouldn't have that kind of stash if not for me."

"You're right, my life is blessed knowing you. I've never had it so good."

"You're always suspicious."

"What's the guy's name you vouched?"

"Anson Beaumont."

"I'll bring twenty grand, that's all."

"I guess," Max said, sounding disappointed. "What a piker you are. Fucking hate dealing with poor people."

"So you want me to draw out twenty thousand dollars, come to Vegas, where it's hot, and get you away from Red Cavanaugh's gorillas. For a minute there I thought this was going to be difficult."

"I knew you'd go for it," said Max, happy to get in the last word.

CHAPTER 3

Max hung up the phone and pushed the curtains back, looked out on the parking lot. There they were, sitting around smoking cigarettes. Couple of Red's Gestapo goons. They were coming in six hour shifts. How the hell did they think he was going to get the money or the guy back with them keeping him bottled up inside his hotel room? He'd given some thought to sneaking out at night but if they saw him, the way these morons thought, it might give them the idea he was trying to skip. At that point, there would be no way to talk himself out of it and they'd take the finger right then.

Fucking Anson caused this, the bastard. Max guaranteed the guy, did him a favor, Anson telling him he couldn't lose and needed the money but instead he could lose and did, putting up a digit when he was light on cash, but losing anyway and then the asshole ran out on him, leaving him to take the weight. So, Max owed the balance.

Red Cavanaugh. Now there was a guy in bad need of anger management when it came to these kind of issues. Cavanaugh had amassed power and a sizable fortune buying up markers around town and loaning money to high rollers. When someone didn't pay on time, Cavanaugh bumped the vig and had his guys hold on to you while Red marked you in some way. His favorite was to pinch the lower lip of the debtor and squeeze until it turned black and blue. You see a puffy lower lip around Vegas you knew the guy owed Red.

So, Max had decided to call Springer though the guy was irritating. What else could he do? Get Springer, who was cagey and tough and maybe the smartest guy Max had ever met. Not smart like he knew math or science or had a high IQ. That wasn't it. No, Springer could think on his feet and the guy's mind was nuclear powered when it came to handling people like Cavanaugh's thugs. The drawback was the guy was hard to read and had a real mouth on him. There would be no way to control Springer once he got there but what was the alternative?

He looked at his hand and wiggled his fingers.

There was no other way.

******

Springer was packing a bag, with Bailey Collins standing around drinking a beer.

"You can't go there. You know that," Bailey said, meaning Vegas. Bailey was Springer's best friend in Aspen. Bailey was a ski instructor along with being a former explosives expert, trained as an airborne ranger.

"In and out," Springer said. "I'll grab Max and get back in time for the weekend."

"Just like that, right?"

"If I don't maybe they'll let me watch while they're cutting Max's finger off. I can see where that might be fun."

"Or they cut your finger off. Give that some thought."

Springer held up a hand and flexed a forefinger a couple of times. Made a face.

Bailey pulled up a kitchen chair and sat backwards on it, his arms over the chair back. "This doesn't sound thought out, which isn't like you. What can you do that the police can't?"

"I don't have any jurisdictional boundaries. Buy him some extra time and I'm not the police so he hasn't turned on anyone. Max is all about Max but he's smart and he makes money for guys like Cavanaugh. They won't kill him." He stopped packing and thought about it for a moment. "Well, maybe they won't, but they might. You never know with them. For the most part they're pretty much bad sports."

Springer kept packing so he wouldn't stop and think about not going. Bailey raised an eyebrow and took a sip of his beer. "Why go help Max, anyway? He's just trouble. He got himself in this mess, let him get himself out."

"He can't get himself out."

"It's a tough life."

Springer kept packing.

"You listen," said Bailey. "But you fail to hear."

"There's that."

"Well," Bailey said, getting up off the chair. "Holler if you need anything. But, just tell me why you're doing this."

"What makes you think I won't enjoy this?"

Bailey crumpled the beer can, shook his head with his eyes closed. "You never learn. Man, when you get in something you go hip-deep, don't you?"

CHAPTER 4

"Too fucking hot for this kinda work," the kid said.

"Have you tried complaining yet?" said Lionel. "Sometimes that works."

"Just saying."

Lionel gave him a look, then ignored him. This kid who couldn't stand not to say everything that was in his head, kept talking, saying, "Why can't we sit inside the bar?"

Lionel swiveled his head towards the kid, looking at him now. "Cause we can't see Max from inside the bar, he decides to go down to the main office and out the back." Shaking his head now, wondering what he had to put up with on this job. He had a fucking business degree and doing this shit. Armando, his usual partner, was in the hospital with a kidney stone so Red sends this kid, a white boy thought he was Tony Montana, Red thinking he was saving money had to use independent guys and punks. "You think about that?"

"He don't pay me to think."

"Be a plus for both of you." Lionel said.

"So, you're gonna bust my balls, that it?"

Lionel Johnson looked at him, not believing how dumb the kid was. Kid in his stupid clothes like he was going on MTV later and holding his gun sideways like he thought real gangsters did, not knowing when you shot that way everything was off and it was hard enough to sight the damned things. Lionel didn't like guns. They were loud, made his ears ring and his eyes blinked when he was shooting anyway so he never got good at it.

Lionel saying now, "Just keep watching and see how long you don't have something stupid to say." Wondering if the kid ever did anything besides shop for bad clothes and listen to his shitty music on his phone, Lionel having to tell him turn it off you gotta be able to hear what's going on. What a black man had to put up with nowadays. White kids who thought they were gangsta rappers.

Lionel had been doing this since he got out of college. Starting off scaring the slow pay crack crazies then getting better work as Casino security before Red upped his pay and the work was better. Now, watching a car with rental plates pull up and a guy get out and walk up to Max's door. "Look here now."

They watched as the door opened and the guy, tall and wide-shouldered, walked inside. Looked like a cop, but managed not to look like one at the same time to Lionel, actually the guy looked like a baseball player. Ten minutes later, the guy came out and walked towards them.

Right towards them.

"Now what do we do?" the kid said, watching the man get closer.

"Keep watching," said Lionel, but wondering what this was about.

******

The way to do it, Springer decided, was to just walk up to the door and bring Max out right in front of them, the two guys he could see now, both of them wearing sports jackets, despite the fact it was 98 in the shade. Springer never liked the heat in Vegas, couldn't understand why anyone would live in such a place which was why he lived in Colorado. He'd been watching the two guys for about an hour before deciding how to do it. One of the guys was a mature black man, knew what he was doing, not acting like he was doing anything but hanging out and a younger guy, edgy and quick in his mannerisms who kept looking around like something *could* happen if he looked hard enough.

He knocked on the motel door, but no one answered. Good, Max was learning to listen a little bit. He'd called him before and told him not to answer the door. "Max, open up. It's me, Springer."

"First you tell me not to answer it and now you want me to answer it." Max complaining already which was his one unchanging trait.

Springer telling him to just open it and when he came inside Max could whine and complain all he wanted. Max saying he was only stating the obvious and this was always the way it went with him, meaning Springer. But, Max opened the door and let Springer in.

"Good move," said Max, flopping down in a chair, a cigarette smoldering in the ash tray on the night stand. "Now we're both stuck inside here. Here's a tip on these things. You might think them out beforehand. Works better."

"This is a no-smoking room, right?"

"Yeah," Max said. "My biggest worry is getting kicked out of the place for smoking while two guys are counting down the minutes to cut my finger off."

"Is your buddy Anson coming with the money?"

"What do you think?"

Springer sat down in one of the motel chairs. Nice room. Furniture was okay, the television was anchored to the chest of drawers. Springer said, "Man, it's hot out there. You couldn't find me a beer could you? And yes, I see the two thugs outside sweating and wishing they were in the bar next door. Way to do it, I were in their place, would be to take turns watching while one of us sat inside the bar, but they're afraid of Cavanaugh, which is the smart thing. It's got to be the heat here, burns everyone's brain where they can't think. Except for you, of course, Max, I know you're thinking clearly. That's why you're holed up in this motel eating room service food. So, what's your plan? I mean, I have one, but you're already criticizing mine before you even hear it which is like you so I'll just sit here and drink beer and listen to how you're going to extricate yourself from this situation."

Max was looking around the room like he couldn't imagine anyone acting this way. "What is it with you? How'd you get like this?"

"You have beer or not?" Springer got up and walked into the kitchenette and opened the refrigerator. There was a six-pack of Budweiser inside, one of them missing. He pulled one out and twisted off the cap and went back and sat down, Max looking at him.

"The fuck's it with you, you come in here already with the lip."

"What are you mad about?" Springer said, wanting Max to suffer a little. He was fun to watch when he was upset. Tipping his beer towards Max and smiling when he did it. "Hot here, isn't it? Don't know how you can stand it."

"I stay inside a lot." Looking around the room now, shaking his head. "You come all this way just to drink beer and make me nervous?"

Springer walked over to the window and stuck a finger in the slats of the Venetian blinds. They needed dusting. "They're out there all right. Saw 'em when I came in. Boy, they look nasty too." He shuddered for effect, having fun. "I think you're right. They're waiting for you."

Max made a face and then shook his head.

Springer said, "I don't think they're shooters. Look like muscle. Maybe the black guy's a shooter but he looks more like a shylock or somebody Cavanaugh sends out to scare people. The other guy? A kid, a little heavy bodied, too much fried food, and boy it'll slow you down. Dressed like it's still the 80's. The black guy looks to be in charge." He stood back a little and smiled at Max. "Hey, I think that's Lionel Johnson. I'm impressed. I remember him from years ago. Sharp guy, we had him on a list of guys to watch when the President came here years ago. 'Known felon', that's what we call then." He smiled at Max and said, "No offense."

"Why do you think you're funny?"

Springer pointed his thumb in the direction of the window. "He was a guy I was supposed to check out. He's no shooter. Lionel is a practical guy for a hoodlum, maybe he'll see how things are, if I explain it to them. The young guy's too agitated and worked up. Probably some wannabe Cavanaugh picked up for this. I've been watching them. Younger guy might shoot without thinking but I don't know. What do you think?"

"I think I gotta get the fuck outta here. It's not just them either, the feds are pissed, too."

"Well, you do have a way about you." Trying to imagine what Max had done to involve federal agents. First things first though. "I think we can get this done but you have to do what I say and no ad-libbing."

Springer looked at him.

Max patted his chest with his fingers. "You don't trust me?"

Springer looked at him thinking it was hard to resist an opening like that, but he was going to leave it alone. Springer leaned back in his chair. "Something else. You're not telling me the whole story. People don't look to collect on a bet then not allow the debtor to pay. Doesn't make sense."

"I thought we been through this. They're degenerate crazoids."

Springer shook his head. "Play it anyway you want. But, you don't tell the truth, I'm walking out without you and you can decide what to do. One way would be wait until dark and try to sneak out but this is Vegas and five'll get you seven they've already paid off the desk clerks and the security people." He nodded his head and said, "Yeah, that's how I see it. You move, then somebody works here can't wait to dial them up on a cell phone. It'll look like you're skipping out and that'll motivate Cavanaugh to cut his losses."

"Okay, okay. What the hell else can I do?"

"Try the truth."

"All right. Just get me out of here first and then I'll tell you what's what." Springer reached into his inside coat pocket and produced a pair of handcuffs. He told Max he was going to cuff him and take him out like he was under arrest. Max protesting as usual, saying why use the cuffs and besides that won't work, these guys'll follow us and when we don't go to the police station they'll know something's up and then they'll wait and it'll be more than just my finger they cut off. Springer telling him to have a little faith and when had he failed him before? Then Max said, you damn near give me ulcers every time I'm around you.

Springer said, "And yet, when you're in trouble, who do you call?" He looked out the window again. "Maybe I talk to them give them a chance to surrender."

"What?" Max put his hand to his forehead, looking sick.

"No, really. It might work they don't shoot me and then come in and shoot you." He held a finger to the Venetian blinds and looked back at Max. "Course, then I'd miss them shooting you and I don't want to miss that."

"I can't tell whether you're crazy or just like to worry me." Looking around now. "Where'd I put my meds? You're a sick man, Springer."

Springer thinking maybe he should have brought ether or a gag. "Max, they're not trying to conceal themselves. What's that tell you?"

"Who knows? They're recidivist imbeciles."

"They're not trying to stop you from going anywhere, they just want to know where you're going. They want to see if you'll lead them to your good friend, Anson, you vouched for. That way they owe you nothing and your buddy's new name is *nine fingers*."

"You mean...?"

"You could've left anytime you wanted. They're not keeping you here, your paranoia is."

"So, take off the cuffs."

"No, I like you this way."

"I don't know a more annoying asshole than you."

Springer thinking he might have to give Max that one.

Even though the men outside knew Max had freedom of movement Springer thought it better to lose them.

Or?

Putting it together now. It could work.

CHAPTER 5

"I been thinking that maybe we follow them if the guy comes out." the kid said to Lionel.

"We just talked about you thinking, right?" said Lionel, but the kid was probably right. Saw the man walk over to a couple of guys and say something to them. Feds? Watching the pair get into a car, Lionel thought the other guy, the one who had cuffed Max, looked familiar. Where had he seen this guy?

And then, something new.

"You believe this?" said Lionel. "The guy's walking right toward us."

"He's fucking stupid then," said the kid.

No, he's not. Lionel remembering the guy now. Cole Springer, two hundred pounds of trouble and mouth.

Lionel stood and said, "This is something here." Springer goes in to Max's room and now looked like he was going to talk to them. About what?

"Don't underestimate this white boy," said Lionel. "Keep your mouth shut and don't let him stir you up. He likes that."

"He fucks with me..."

"And he will and you will keep your dick holster shut. Honest to god, don't say a fucking word or I'll tell Red to sew your lips shut. Red likes that you know."

"Why do you talk to me like that?"

"Just listen. This man is a pain in the ass and loves being one. Ignore him."

"Hey fellas," said Springer, getting closer. "Man, it's hot out here today. I were you I'd duck into that bar." Nodding in the direction of the bar. "Cold beer sounds good, doesn't it? You seem a little over-dressed."

"What do you want, Springer?" said Lionel.

"Is that you, Lionel? You look like you put on some weight."

"I eat good. Red sends his love."

"He's a lovely man. Who's the child?"

"Who you calling a 'child'?" said the kid.

Lionel could feel his sphincter tighten. Fucking kid. Never listens.

"Not you, fatty. You look post-pubescent."

"I don't..."

Lionel held up a hand to the kid, "What did I tell you?"

Springer said, "Listen, Lionel, I need your help on something."

Lionel relaxed, saying, "Don't know what there could be I could do for you. I ain't exactly in the helping business. I'm more in the fuck people over business. You want some of that?"

"In a couple minutes I'm going to take Max somewhere away from here and I'd appreciate if you'd allow it. He skipped on a bond back in Colorado and I'm taking him back. I'm getting paid to do this. You know how it is."

"Is he fucking kidding?" said the kid, not knowing how to talk or seeing how it was.

"What happens we don't allow such?" said Lionel.

"See, that's the thing," said Springer, "I'm really wanting you to feel like you have some say in this. You know, like we were agreeing on it."

Lionel thinking Springer was a guy didn't look like much, sort of moved like an athlete and you could mistake him for a citizen real easy but Lionel knew the guy's reputation.

"You come out with Max," the kid was saying, "and it'll be a fucking mistake, asshole."

Springer looking at the kid, like he just noticed him, then back at Lionel. The man knowing who was in charge without asking. Lionel put a hand out again to the kid so he wouldn't escalate things. Here's a boy not smart enough to realize when a man walks up cool like this was somebody had things under control. Lionel said, "I'm thinking on this scenario we have before us. You're here to take Max out, right? However, we're supposed to sit on him until he comes out, see? We have to keep him in our view until he meets a deadline. When he comes out we're supposed to take him someplace until Red can talk to him. You can understand our position."

"Why not just go in and take him right away?"

"It ain't nothing to you," said the kid, Lionel weary from hearing him talk. "You just need to get on down the road."

Springer looked at the kid, this time different, then again at Lionel. "Am I talking to you or this?" He nodded his head sideways at the kid.

"That's fucking it," said the kid. That's when the gun came out of the Springer's pocket, or from somewhere. It was quick, almost like he'd made it appear in his hand. Lionel sucked in a breath.

"So, you're going to make me shoot you. That what you want?" Springer said. "I can shoot you now or wait until I take Max out and you try to stop me. Up to you."

The kid's eyes got big, not believing this was happening. Hell, Lionel not believing it his own self. The man comes on affable, folksy, that next-door neighbor maneuver going for him and then the other side of him could surprise you. Lionel said, "Red's out of town and he doesn't trust Max." Springer nodded, smiling. The guy understanding about Max and now telling Lionel, so you think he'll run and Red will have to look for him? Lionel said that was right and he had to know how Red was when he was pissed off and that's no good for anybody you have to believe that. Now the man shrugging and saying how it was the way it was going to be and why not make it easier on everybody?

The kid interrupting again. "This is fucked-up." To Lionel he said, "You're not buying into this, are you?" Lionel shrugged, pointed at the gun in the man's hand, said, "Man, why don't you swallow a big spoonful of 'shut-the-fuck-up. You have to factor in this man's got the gun. You *do* see it don't you? You can't have every fucking thing your way."

The kid looking at Springer now, relaxing his shoulders, giving Springer a tough guy slouch, Lionel not believing the kid was taking an attitude but this is how they learned. The kid said, "You make a move with Max and we'll see if you're bad enough."

Springer looked at the kid, his eyes level but his face unchanged. "Look. I'm going to talk to Lionel here and then after I'm done you can scare me to death some more. But, I hear another word out of you before then," Springer said, scratching his cheek with a finger, "and I'm going to hit you in the throat."

"You can't," the kid began before the man slapped him across the throat with the same hand he'd been scratching his cheek with. Made Lionel flinch it happen so fast.

So, here's the scene, the kid leaning over now, hands to his throat, hacking and trying to breathe, Lionel shaking his head and the man shrugging, the gun still in his hand but not really pointing at anything. "I tried to tell him." Like he was explaining why he did it. "You heard me tell him, didn't you? He should've listened."

Lionel nodded, shrugged, looking at the kid bent over. "This kid ain't learned shit since I've been around him. He's like the antidote for intelligence."

"I'm bringing Max out and I don't want any trouble. If there is I will shoot you and Sparky there. I won't like it but I'll do it." The man looked at the kid, who was choking and spittle hanging from his lips, grossing Lionel out. "Maybe not shoot you." Springer smiling at Lionel. "But, I may shoot him more than once, give him something to think about." Then he looked Lionel straight in the face and said, "Also, see those two guys over there?" Nodding in the direction of the two men Lionel had seen Springer talking to before. "What's it going to be, Lionel? Easy or hard?"

"You know how it is. It's the job."

"I'll guarantee Red gets his money. Let me get Max to a safe place and then I'll get the money out of him or pay it myself. My word on it. How's that?"

"Well," said Lionel, looking at the kid and telling him, "stand up and raise your arms. Opens the diaphragm. Helps you breathe. Shit. That looks bad, all bent over like that. Boy, have some pride." Then to Springer he said, "Easy works best for me. What about the finger?"

Springer shaking his head. "Nope."

Lionel puffed out his cheeks and exhaled. "Not even that, huh? What about Red? You're gonna go and piss him off, you know. Make my working conditions worse."

"You figure there's any chance he's going to like me better I walk away from this?"

Lionel smiled. "Hell no."

"It's not like he's sending me Christmas cards now."

"'Spose not."

Springer put the gun away, winked at Lionel and walked back to the hotel. Five minutes later, the dude and Max got into a rental car and drove away. Right after that one of the guys that the man had talked to left in a taxi. The other guy continued to stand there. Lionel, being the curious type, walked over to the other guy and asked how he knew the guy. Asked what his name was.

The guy looked at Lionel like Lionel's lost his mind and said, "Never saw the guy in my life. He just said you were friends of his and was going to play a joke on you. Told us to look your direction and then not look at you again." Lionel made a face and the guy said, "He said it was a joke, but I don't get it. What was funny about any of this?"

"Funny to him, I guess," said Lionel.

Lionel smiled. Springer just walked away with Max Shapiro right in front of them. Hard not to like the bold motherfucker. Cole Springer. He was cool. No doubt about it.

IF YOU LIKED THIS, CHECK OUT THE COLE SPRINGER TRILOGY

COLE SPRINGER HAS A MUSICAL SOUL, A QUICK WIT AND A CON-MAN'S MIND.

Ex-Secret Service agent, Cole Springer, has exchanged his badge for a piano and the high-altitude life of Aspen, Colorado but has not lost his appetite for danger.

Springer delights in playing button men and gangsters for personal gain and amusement. Springer, while an affable man, is double tough, hard to kill and has an ironic sense of humor. His girlfriend, determined CBI agent Tobi Ryder, doesn't know whether to love him, forget him, or arrest him for his escapades that skirt the edges of law...

The Cole Springer Trilogy includes: Springer's Gambit, Springer's Longshot and Springer's Fortune.

AVAILABLE NOW ON AMAZON

ABOUT THE AUTHOR

W.L. Ripley is the author of the critically acclaimed Wyatt Storme and Cole Springer mystery-thriller series' featuring modern knight errant Wyatt Storme, and Maverick ex-secret service agent, Cole Springer.

W.L. Ripley is a lifetime Missouri resident who has been a sportswriter, award-winning career educator and NCAA Div. II basketball coach. Ripley enjoys watching football, golf, and spending time with friends and family. He's a father, grandfather, and unapologetic Schnauzer lover.

In addition to the Storme & Springer series, Ripley has crafted two new series' heroes – Jake Morgan (Home Fires) and Conner McBride (McBride Doubles Down) for Wolfpack Publishing. Wolfpack is reissuing the Cole Springer series and Ripley is developing a new Cole Springer thriller for Wolfpack.

ABOUT THE AUTHOR

CPSIA information can be obtained
at www.ICGtesting.com
Printed in the USA
LVHW040104110921
697540LV00007B/531

9 781639 770090